Good Old Boy
and the
Witch of Yazoo

To Sara and Johnny and Commander Russell Blair,
and to Lyn Covington

Good Old Boy
and the
Witch of Yazoo

by

Willie Morris

Yoknapatawpha Press
OXFORD, MISSISSIPPI

GOOD OLD BOY AND THE WITCH OF YAZOO

Copyright © 1989 by Willie Morris

Published by Yoknapatawpha Press
P.O. Box 248, Oxford, MS 38655

ISBN 0-916242-67-6 Library of Congress 89-51149

Book design by Lawrence Wells
Printed in the United States of America

Double, double toil and trouble,
Fire burn and caldron bubble.
Fillet of a fenny snake,
In the caldron boil and bake.
Eye of newt and toe of frog,
Wool of bat and tongue of dog,
Adder's fork and blindworm's sting,
Lizard's leg and howlet's wing,
For a charm of powerful trouble,
Like a Hell broth boil and bubble.

Macbeth

Author's Foreword

When we last left the good old boys—and the beloved girl, Rivers Applewhite—they had solved the terrible enigma of the Clark Mansion, having done so at the risk of their very lives. In venturing to the Mansion on that dark, stormy night in the great Delta they had been both frightened and brave, not at all an unusual emotion among the human breed. Even in those days they had a feeling they were growing up. They wanted to, and then again they didn't. Surely this is the way people are, and have always been, even before television, electricity, jet airplanes and the telephone. You want to grow older, and yet you don't. Isn't this strange? Can anyone explain it?

I did not plan to write a sequel to *Good Old Boy*. I was getting older myself and was reluctant to revive those ponderous fears and tender hallucinations of that vanished time, for they dwell yet in my deepest dreams. I also did not wish to disturb the languid old tranquillity of the town, paused in that instant between its unhurried isolation and the coming of the television, and the shopping malls, and the wealthy "subdivisions" without sidewalks, and the big monster highways and the innocence lost. Three things changed my mind.

First, the Walt Disney people filmed a movie of *Good Old Boy* in Mississippi. Millions of children saw it, I was told. Ryan Francis, the young Hollywood actor who played "Little Willie," wrote me from California: "Please, Big Willie, write another book where I can play you again, and where Rivers and I are one year older. I want to come back to the South and go fishing and see the bugs in summer."

Second, thousands of children from all over America wrote me that they wanted to know what happened in the lives of Willie, Rivers, Spit, Bubba, Henjie, Billy, Old Skip and the others. Do experiences have a way of sustaining themselves? my young correspondents asked. Were there further adventures they should know about?

Finally, one night at the kitchen table of William Faulkner's mother's house in Mississippi, the sounds and stirrings of the springtime all around, my friends and publishers Deanie and Larry of the Yoknapatawpha Press, knowing my trepidations on renewing those scary, tempestuous *Good Old Boy* days, confronted me: "You must tell it once more. What are you—a man or a mouse?"

So I return one last time to those faraway moments. One year makes a difference. My children are leaving me. I wish they would stay still forever. Sometimes at somnolent twilight dusks, the Dixie air orange and sibilant and the cicadas singing their songs, I feel the blind impassioned passing of time, and I am sad. Come back, Rivers! Come back, Willie! Come back, Old Skip! Come back all of us!

W.M.
Oxford, Mississippi
June, 1989

One

IT MUST HAVE STILL been strange to see an English smooth-haired fox terrier driving a Ford Model-A roadster up Main Street in the Year of Our Lord 1946. Yet the old men sitting in the decrepit cane bottom chairs in front of the Jones Feed and Seed Store and whittling hickory sticks with their Barlow knives scarcely looked up.

"I told you it wouldn't work, Willie," Henjie complained. As always, he and Bubba had slid down out of sight in the front seat next to me. I was scrunched low behind the wheel, steering the car while my dog Old Skip sat in my lap with his front paws balanced on the wheel.

"They ain't even looking," Billy said from the rumble seat in the rear.

"You been to the well too often," Bubba agreed. He sat up and glanced back at the feed store.

I didn't say anything but I sat up, too. I was chagrined. Skip turned the driving back over to me. I was not old enough yet to have my driver's license, but the Yazoo Po-

1

lice Department usually let us boys practice driving if we were careful and watched the road. This of course did not include letting dogs drive. Not a single dog in town had a driver's 'license yet.

I stopped for the traffic light across from the courthouse and saw Mrs. Annie Laurie Stillwater and her tattle-tale daughter Edith in their Dodge coming toward us.

"I'm gonna try it again," I said. "Y'all get down!"

I put Skip up in my lap with his paws on the wheel, and my friends slumped down out of sight. Peering over the dashboard I saw Edith recognize us, but when the light changed she passed by us without another glance. She just sat there looking disdainfully ahead. I sat up once more and pushed Skip over to the middle of the seat. It wasn't his fault that the trick wasn't working. I drove down by the stockyard and slaughter house beyond the bend in the river and pulled over.

"When a dog driving a car down Main Street on April Fool's Day don't get one little bit of attention," I said, "something *is* wrong."

It was one of those dry, cool days in the Delta when the air, paused ever so poignantly at the cusp of things, can't seem to make up its mind whether it's spring or summer. The pink azaleas and forsythia were blooming and the trees were lushly budding and a soft tender laziness pervaded everything. The war was over, and the soldiers had come home after fighting in Germany or the Pacific and now, in April of '46, had finally stopped wearing their uniforms around town. They'd marched in the victory parades and told their stories and were ready to get back to their law practices and cotton gins and drugstores and farms. But where did that leave us good old boys? We'd missed World War Two.

"There ain't nothing going on," I said.

"*Baseball* season's started," Billy said.

"The Yankees are picked to win again," Henjie said,

trying as best he could to start an argument with me. Everybody knew I was a Cardinals fan like my father, Ray, since the Cards were the closest to us in St. Louis.

But I wasn't interested in baseball. At least not just then. I was about to turn the car around and drive back through town, not going anywhere but just driving, when Billy pointed at the open door of the Yazoo Slaughter House.

"What's that?" he said.

We could see the great sides of beef hanging on hooks suspended from the rafters, freshly cut and still dripping. We couldn't help staring. I pulled over to the curb.

"Is that a washtub of *blood* under that carcass?" Bubba said. "Look how *dark* it is."

"Boy, if we were vampires wouldn't we have fun!" Billy said.

"Yeechh," Henjie said.

"Wait a minute," I said. "I got an idea."

We got out of Bubba's car—his father gave it to him when he was nine—and left Skip inside. I didn't want him licking the slaughter house floor. Too much blood's not good for a dog, especially a dog not all that used to blood.

Ordinarily we didn't poke around the slaughter house much, although we'd explored it along with just about every other building in Yazoo. The slaughter house was not a place you wanted to devote much time to. It had a rancid, unholy smell, and the wooden floor was black with dried blood. They slaughtered cattle and hogs to sell to meat packers and chain groceries in Jackson, our state capital, 42 miles away.

Bubba was right. There *was* a big bucket lipping full of cow's blood so dark it was almost ebony. We stared at that melancholy liquid, feeling weird to see so much of it at once, sort of hypnotized by it. The smell was so thick and strong that I held my breath. I imagine we all were doing it, too, though none of us would've admitted it.

I looked around. Nobody else was in sight. Mr. Howell,

who ran the slaughter house and always wore a bloody white apron, must've stepped out to get a Coke or to smoke a cigarette.

"Come on," I said. "Let's find us some cans."

"What for?" Bubba said.

"We need that blood."

"What for?" Billy repeated.

"I don't know, but we can't just leave it here going to waste," I said.

Henjie found two empty gallon cans out back of the slaughter house, and we filled them nearly full. When Bubba and I tilted the bucket over to pour the blood, some of it splashed on my tennis shoes.

"Will that wash off?" Billy said.

"I hope not," I said.

We hoisted the cans into the rumble seat of Bubba's car, and this time Bubba drove while I sat in the back with Old Skip. I needed to think.

"Where are we going?" Bubba asked.

"The Clark Mansion," I said.

Everybody got quiet except for Skip: he was so smart he began to pant in anticipation. I never knew a dog who liked trouble so much. Nearly a year had passed since the police broke up the gang of giant Indians who had been robbing graves and hiding the coffins at the old Clark Mansion. The collapsed, abandoned house out in the Delta, dire as a forlorn dream, had lost most of its terror for the boys and girls of Yazoo. However, when Bubba turned down the dirt road that cut across cotton fields lined with wispy, impoverished bolls still clinging to the stubble, I felt a thrill course down my spine. We all craned our necks to catch the first glimpse of the house around the bend where tall, otherworldly trees hung over the spectral winding lane. It was like seeing a face appear suddenly at a lonesome window.

There the old house stood, two stories tall, its white paint long faded and peeling, leaning slightly to one side where rot and termites had undermined the foundation, waiting for a storm to knock it over. You could almost imagine the echoes of the departed Indians from inside, envision too the dank secret passageways we had discovered back then in our evanescent moment of glory. Bubba stopped the car in front of the house, but for a minute nobody got out. We could hear the early springtime breeze sighing through the filthy broken windows, like a throaty voice whispering.

Yet the birds and wasps flying in and out of the eaves weren't ghosts. The enormous oak branch that had grown up under the roof and partly lifted it up like a can being split asunder was no apparition. And the seven-foot tall Indians had long since run off and were nowhere to be seen.

There was a rumor that they'd left Mississippi and were hiding out with their Choctaw relatives in Oklahoma. Maybe they struck it rich in the oil business and were living like royalty out west. Maybe they were playing basketball for the University of Oklahoma. No one really knew. They'd vanished from the earth, and I say good riddance.

We got out of the Model-A. I was removing the first container of blood when I heard a moaning sound that was not caused by anything as simple as the wind. We stood bunched together looking around, like spiders in a tangle. Skip immediately started sniffing the ground, then trotted with aroused purpose toward the house.

"What was that?" Billy said.

"It's just the *Yazoo*," Bubba said. "Just the water rushing over a log jam."

He nodded his head in the direction of the Yazoo River, which wound around the Clark plantation, tawny and serpentine in the fragile April mist. Then the moan came again, and it wasn't rushing water.

"What was *that*?" Bubba said.

"It came from the Mansion!" Henjie said.

5

Nobody moved. Then Skip began to bark. He'd found something behind the house. What was it?

"It could be a bobcat," Henjie said.

"Or a panther," Billy said.

"It could be *anything*," Bubba said.

We couldn't get in the car and leave Skip to the mercies of voracious Delta beasts. I stood there uncertainly, holding the can of blood at my side. Maybe if I threw it on the ground that would distract whatever it was, long enough for us to get away.

"Come here, Skip!" I called softly. "Come here, boy."

Skip didn't stop barking, but now he started backing up, his back legs moving gingerly in reverse. Something was coming toward us. We could hear blackberry thorns scratching against its legs.

"Spit McGee!" Bubba and Henjie exclaimed together.

Spit stepped out of the bushes with a broad waggish grin. He carried a shotgun over his shoulder. A dead 'possum hung from his worn leather belt. Spit was half a year older than we. He was taller, too, and skinny as a straw. He'd lived in the swamps for as long as I remembered and knew about things not found in books. In his eternal boondocks resourcefulness, as the reader may recall, he'd saved us that earlier night in this very Clark Mansion, just as we thought we were done for. He was so proud of the fuzz on his chin that he let it grow to a quarter of an inch, although you couldn't see it unless you got close. He'd let you feel it for a nickel.

"Scared you, didn't I?" Spit said.

"Naw!" Billy spoke up. "Willie wanted to see if Skip'd tree you, that's all."

"Where you been, McGee?" Bubba said. "You gonna have to repeat the seventh grade if you don't come back to school."

"Maybe I will, maybe I won't," Spit said. "I'll lead the seventh grade to the state championship in all sports."

"What you been doing?" Billy said.

"Nothin'. Just settin' out trotlines. Whatcha doing with that *blood* ?"

"Nothin'. Just leaving mystic signs," I said.

"*What* signs?" Spit asked.

Everybody glanced appraisingly at me. I hadn't known what we were going to do with the blood until that very minute.

"Mystic signs," I repeated.

"What's that?" Henjie said.

"You know, like witches and stuff," Bubba said, making out for all the world that he knew precisely what was going on.

"What's the point?" Henjie said.

"If you have to ask, you might as well forget it," Bubba said.

"Well, I mean, nobody comes out here anymore," Henjie argued, puffing up his cheeks a little, so that for the moment he resembled a precocious fortune-teller over a milky crystal ball. "How's anybody gonna know about it?"

"Oh, they'll find out," I said.

"What's that, cow's blood?" Spit leaned over and sniffed the can. "Whoo-ee, that's rank. You get it at the slaughter house? Well, you can't get very mystic with one can of blood. It won't stretch far enough."

"We got another can in the car!" Billy said.

"What kinda signs did you have in mind?" Spit asked me.

"I don't know. Something weird, I guess." To be truthful I'd not completely thought out a plan.

"How 'bout a star inside a circle?" Spit said.

"What's that?" I said.

"Sign of a witch," he said, nonchalant as could be. "We could paint it on the side of the house over there, where people could see it good."

"A star in a circle? How'd you know *that*?" I asked curi-

7

ously. Spit always had a habit of taking over my ideas, though I had to admit he usually came up with some deft and intriguing ones.

"I don't know," he said. "Read about it somewheres. Or somebody told me. Whatta you say?"

We looked sideways at each other. Nobody wanted the others to think he was reluctant to get into trouble.

"It's okay with me," I said with a shrug.

"Me, too," Bubba said.

"Me, three," Henjie and Billy both said.

We fetched the other can of blood and set both of them on the rotting front porch which had caved in mightily on one side. Spit left and returned with an old paint brush from a defunct shed. The bristles were stiff, but after we dipped it in the blood they softened up.

"You gonna play with that blood or paint with it?" Spit asked. "Bubba and Henjie, you lift Billy up on your shoulders so he can paint the star. Remember, Billy, it has to be big enough to see from a long ways off. People gonna be *scared* to get close to the Clark Mansion after this. Scareder than ever."

Bubba and Henjie let Billy climb on their shoulders and gripped his legs while he dipped the brush. I held the can as he painted a star on the front of the house about four or five feet high. Before he completed the circle around it we realized he was dripping blood on all of us except Spit, who was standing safely behind us giving instructions, as was his usual wont. We had blood in our hair, on our faces and our clothes. By the time Billy finished we looked like we'd been in a battle with the Nazi *Wehrmacht* .

We stood back to inspect the witch's star. It looked strange. The blood was already turning black and attracting wicked horseflies. Nobody said a word.

"Ack-ack-ack-ack!" Billy made the sounds of a machine gun, and Bubba clutched his stomach and pretended to expire of an agonized death. So we messed around for a while

8

playing World War Two and the assassinations of Baby
Face Nelson and John Dillinger until Spit said we'd better
jump in the Yazoo River and wash the blood off before the
stain set in. He took an old bar of soap out of the same shed
behind the house. The soap was brown with dust and
hadn't been used for years.

"Where'd this *soap* come from?" I said.

Everybody knew about Spit's aversion to taking baths.
He didn't hate bathing any more than the rest of us. He
was just better at avoiding it.

"It's for emergencies," he said.

Spit led us down a deer trail to the river. On the way
there he showed us deer tracks and quail nests and some
cottonmouth moccasin skins. He knew every fishing hole
and sunken log where the big channel catfish lived and
rabbit patch and coon hollow in Yazoo County. When Spit
McGee talked, we listened.

We stripped off and went for a swim in the River of
Death. That's what the Choctaw Indian word *Yazoo* means.
You didn't forget that too easily. The water was piercingly
cold, but we got used to it pretty quick by ducking each
other and having some serious water fights. We were able
to wash most of the blood off. What we couldn't scrub out
we decided to call bird's blood. We'd say we'd been hunting
snowbirds and had cleaned them for Spit to cook in a stew.
Snowbirds migrated north every spring and were a fine
nuisance roosting in trees all over town and covering people's yards with their inane droppings. We had snowbird
hunts with B-B rifles. I once killed two with one shot but I
felt bad about it, later.

Spit built a fire, and we hung our clothes on sticks
nearby to dry them off. Skip treed a squirrel and Spit shot
at it but missed. Skip kept circling the tree, barking his
head off. I never saw Old Skip so happy and proud.

After our clothes were more or less dry, we got dressed
again.

9

"What if nobody finds out about our sign and this is all for nothing?" Bubba said.

"Yeah," Billy said, "not many people come out here."

"People will find out," I said.

"How?" Bubba said.

"The word will get around," I said. "Remember, Memphis wasn't built in a day."

When we returned to the Clark Mansion there wasn't much sun left. The circled star had faded a little but it had a curious kind of shine, even in the grey, shimmering light of dusk. It was eerie.

I felt a shiver go up my neck, and when I glanced at my friends I knew they felt the same way.

"It's some joke the sun's playing," Henjie said.

"Yeah, some kind of reflection." Bubba looked around hopefully.

"Like when the clouds in the east turn pink after the sun's gone down," Henjie said.

"Look at it glow," Billy whispered.

"Well," Spit said, "that's what mystic's all about, ain't it?"

"We better be gettin' home," Bubba said. "It's nearly dark."

We threw away the empty cans in a glade of trees and underbrush and told Spit so long. If we got home after dark our mothers would ask questions. We pledged Spit to secrecy and asked him to come back to school and play shortstop in our crucial game against Belzoni Junior High. Then we got in the car, and Bubba started the motor and drove away from the Mansion.

When we reached the first bend in the road Bubba slowed down so we could look back. We could see the circled star shining against the grim weathered boards with its strange vivid incandescence. It was so quiet in the car that

10

I could hear Skip panting again. He wagged his tail as if hoping we were still looking for squirrels.

"*Must* be some trick of the light," Billy said ominously.

"Yeah," Henjie said. "Must be."

Two

"NUMBER PLEASE," THE OPERATOR said.

"Two-three-seven," I said, disguising my voice to sound deep and husky, like the radio announcers from New York. I listened to the phone ring once, twice.

"Hello?"

"Miss Abbott?"

"Yes, who is this?"

"Never mind that. A sign awaits you at the Clark Mansion."

I hung up and looked at Bubba. Through the plate-glass window of his parents' den we could see Henjie and Billy tossing a baseball back and forth on the lawn. This was the fifth phonecall we'd made to Yazoo's five worst gossips, based on our own informal poll. We decided we didn't need to phone any more than these five ladies to get the news around. Here's our list:

> *Mrs. Snellgrove*–spreads stories and gossip mainly at
> Piggly Wiggly store. (10-12 contacts)

Mrs. Hathaway –tells everybody at First Baptist Church (150 contacts on Sunday or 25 at Wednesday prayer meeting)

Mrs. Kolb–(#1) works at Post Office (maybe 250 contacts on a good day)

Mrs. Dawson–invalid widow in wheelchair, spends all day on phone (30 contacts)

Miss Abbott–Old Maid schoolteacher, has nothing to do but gossip (15 contacts, including principal and school janitor)

"Who do you think will call first?" I asked.

"Miz Dawson," Bubba said.

"I'll bet you a Dr. Pepper it's Miss Abbott."

"It's a bet," Bubba said. "But why her?"

"'Cause it's Saturday," I said.

The phone rang. Bubba answered. He looked at me and raised his eyebrows. "No'm, she ain't–I mean, she isn't here, Miss Abbott. Yes'm, I'll tell her to call you."

I signaled to Bubba and pretended to scribble a message.

"Oh," Bubba added, "would you like to leave a message? Uh-huh. Uh-huh. At the Clark Mansion? Yes'm, I'll be sure to tell her. 'Bye." Bubba hung up and looked at me. "Morris, how'd you know?"

"Saturdays get pretty long for the Miss Abbotts of this world," I said sagely. "She can't wait for school to start again on Monday so she can be mean to everybody. Anyway, it's working. Let's go tell Billy and Henjie."

A traffic jam formed on the lane leading to the Clark Mansion. Bubba and I sat in the back seat of my daddy's green Desoto and tried to keep from laughing as my mother drove off the road and back on again to maneuver closer to the forbidding old house. People were getting out of their cars and trampling the weeds in front of the Mansion, gawking at the circled star painted in blood and talking about it in agitated little whispers.

"Look at that," Mama said. "Isn't that just *awful* ?"

13

Bubba and I couldn't so much as glance at each other for fear of bursting out laughing. Spit McGee's idea had worked even better than we'd hoped. I could've bear-hugged old Spit.

"Hooliganism's not funny," Mama said over her shoulder as she turned the car around and drove back toward town. "Promise me you boys will stay away from such shenanigans."

"Yes, ma'am," we lied in unison.

Driving into town, Mama slowed down as we passed the City Waterworks Building. "I wonder what *that's* all about?" she said.

Bubba and I followed her troubled glance to see a crowd gathered around the goldfish pool at the base of the water tower. The sheriff's car was parked nearby. We got out of the Desoto and went to see what was going on. Bubba and I eased through the crowd obliquely and squatted on the front row. The sheriff was fishing a dead crow out of the goldfish pool. On the brick wall around the pool someone had painted another star within a circle, along with an incomprehensible Latin phrase. The Catholic priest, Father O'Hara, dipped his handkerchief in the fountain and started rubbing out the words, which clearly had been printed in blood. Before he erased it I saw what it said:

VENUM DAEMONUS

"What's *that* mean!" Bubba whispered to me.

"Something in Latin," I said, shrugging.

I shivered to myself. Who's out there? I thought. Who in Yazoo knows Latin like this? On both sides of the foreign message were these little upside down crosses and the number 666. What did *that* mean?

"Let's ask Father O'Hara," Bubba said.

"It's nonsense!" The priest turned and stared at us, having overheard Bubba. "Pure nonsense, boys. Don't put any stock in such mischief."

14

"Okay, Father," I said, "but what does *venum daemonus* mean?"

"Tomorrow's the Sabbath." The Father ignored my question and continued rubbing out the letters painted in blood and muttering to himself, "It won't do for people to see signs like this on a holy day—or *any* day."

I noticed Mr. Mott, editor and publisher of the *Yazoo Herald*, wandering up with his big black camera in hand.

"Just a minute, Father," Mr. Mott said. "I'd like to get a picture of it first."

Father O'Hara stubbornly kept on rubbing out the letters. "Should our congregations be reading about devil worship?" he said over his shoulder. "What good will publishing trash like this do? Won't that merely play into the hands of the demonologists, whoever they are?"

Devil worship? I thought. *Demonologists?*

"Holy cow! This is the real McCoy," I whispered to Bubba.

"Freedom of the press, Father," Mr. Mott argued. "The First Amendment. My readers have a right to know what's going on."

"Well, in my humble opinion," Father O'Hara shook his finger at Mr. Mott, "you'll only add fuel to the fire. Next, people will be saying the Witch of Yazoo has returned to haunt them."

The Witch of Yazoo! I thought.

"That's it," I said to Bubba, drawing him off to the side.

"What is?" he said.

"Who does everybody think is a witch?" I asked him.

"That's easy. Miss Eddie Mack, because she's the original Witch's great-granddaughter."

Bubba was referring to Yazoo's infamous Witch, who on May 25, 1904, was widely reputed to have escaped from the grave to burn the whole town down. The chains over her grave were discovered broken on that fateful day. "Miss Eddie Mack" was Edwina McBride, a descendant of

15

the legendary Witch and a pretty suspicious person herself.

"What are you getting at?" Bubba said.

"If anybody in town knows what's going on," I replied, "Miss Eddie Mack does."

I watched Father O'Hara scrub the bloodstains until they were nearly gone. He'd ruined his handkerchief but he didn't seem to care. Being a Methodist myself I was slightly in awe of Father O'Hara and the little Catholic church in Yazoo. I wondered what the priest thought about these signs. Did he know something that the rest of us didn't?

Bubba and I started walking up Grand Avenue together.

"You think Miss Eddie Mack killed that crow and wrote those signs?" Bubba said.

"If she didn't, I bet she knows who did."

"Wait a minute. Where are we going?" Bubba said.

"Witch's Hill," I said.

"Uh-uh, not me!" He paused on the sidewalk. "I'm not going up there, not after what's happened."

"You scared?" I meant to dare Bubba to come with me. Quite frankly I didn't want to go to Miss Eddie Mack's house by myself. Would you?

"That place gives me the heebie-jeebies," Bubba said. "If that's being scared, then I'm scared. You go by yourself if you want to."

"Something's going on," I persisted, "and we got to get to the bottom of it."

"*You* get to the bottom of it," Bubba said. "I'm going home."

16

Three

I DECIDED TO CUT across the cemetery on the way to Miss Eddie Mack's house. Ordinarily I wasn't too afraid of being in the cemetery—in the daytime, that is—but that afternoon there was something dreadfully spooky about the light, much as it had glimmered at the Clark Mansion after we painted the sign. The early spring wildflowers danced grotesquely in a murmuring breeze. A dog howled from the farthest distance. The shadows of the tombstones appeared to move as I walked past, as if the very grave markers themselves were watching me, as if the sleeping dead were restive and complaining. I started walking faster and, while glancing apprehensively over my shoulder, tripped and fell. When I looked up there was a crow sitting on a tombstone and I was lying on top of a broken chain.

It was the Witch's grave .

I leapt up but the crow didn't fly away. It sat there looking directly at me. I was so scared I froze, and I looked at it from a sideways angle. Then I realized that it was dead.

Somebody had propped it up on top of the Witch's tombstone as if it were alive.

I started running and didn't stop until I got far away from the graves. I paused to listen—what did I expect to hear, a crow calling?—but the only sound was the beating of my own vainglorious heart, *thump, thump, thump.* I took a deep breath. I couldn't let a dead crow scare me, could I?

Probably just some kids playing, I told myself. Kids'll do just about anything.

Miss Eddie Mack's house stood on the crest of the hill. The sidewalk ended before it reached the top, and the pavement also ran out as it approached her house. On one side of the road was a wild tossing ravine covered with the creeping kudzu. On the other was a wooded hill that sloped down to the cemetery. I sneaked up to a privet hedge in front of her house and peered over it.

Everything about her house was crooked, from the brick chimney that leaned over the roof to the sheds attached to the main building at foolish random. Roofed walkways going to garage, barn and toolshed gave the place an octopus kind of shape. Windows set at odd angles made the entire dwelling look like a sad-eyed monster.

I'd never seen Miss Eddie Mack's house except when I was moving fast. Now that I had time to observe it, I think I kind of liked it. It had a certain *character*. There was nothing else remotely like it in all of Yazoo.

Miss Eddie Mack had been married twice. Both of her husbands died—in their prime, people said—and left her a rich woman. The cause of their deaths was unknown. Poison, some said.

In front of her house was a bottle tree, which was what the black people of Yazoo called a dead tree with empty glass bottles of all sizes and shapes and colors stuck on the ends of the branches. Bubba's parents' maid, Ruby, had told me this was ancient voodoo magic brought here by African slaves. The bottles were used to capture evil spirits in the

18

night, who crawled into them and couldn't get out. Their magic then belonged to the person who had caught them and he or she could turn it from bad to good—Ruby said. It made sense to Ruby, and to me, too.

Looking at the unnatural bottle tree outlined against the sky with its many-colored glass "leaves," I could almost envision little lights glinting inside the bottles—like the lightning bugs we liked to put in jars—as evil spirits spun round and round, searching for an escape. Then I imagined what it would be like if I were trapped in one of those bottles, my fingers sliding against the slippery smooth surface, my cries muffled from within.

"Boy, what are you doing!"

I nearly jumped out of my skin. Miss Eddie Mack had come up behind me so quietly.

"Nothing, ma'am," I said.

"Don't you nothin' *me*! You're up to somethin' or you wouldn't *be* here. Aren't you Ray Morris' boy?"

"Yes'm."

So she knew who I was and yet—people said—she ignored what went on in town.

"What do they call you?"

"Willie."

"Well, Willie, does your daddy know you're up here spying on me?"

"No, ma'am. I mean, I'm *not* spying."

"Of course you are. I saw you peeping over my hedge. But seeing that you've come all this way, you might as well come inside and satisfy your curiosity, or else you'll be back. Isn't that right?"

Before I could reply she'd gone through an opening in the hedge and was walking toward the house. I reluctantly followed her down a narrow, verdant path through a yard full of weeds in full April bloom: milkweed, rabbit tobacco, cockleburs, bitterweed and goldenrod. Everything except the bitterweed smelled good. I appraised Miss Eddie Mack

19

while she wasn't looking at me. She wasn't as old as I expected. She had grey hair, all right, but her skin was smooth, and she was youthful and energetic. She walked with quick little steps as though marching.

The front door creaked a little when we went in, and standing in a small modest foyer I immediately detected an unusual scent—not dusty or musty but rather spicey, a Christmas kind of smell, as though everything had been sprinkled with nutmeg or cinnamon.

"I grow herbs," Miss Eddie Mack said, as if divining my own thoughts. I turned away to disguise my amazement and saw potted plants in every window, on shelves against the walls—anywhere they could catch the light.

Miss Eddie Mack gave me a guided tour of her indoor herb "garden," listing the various plants as we came to them: alfalfa, sage, thyme and dill, among others. I couldn't remember all the names. I noticed that her house was cluttered with odd pieces of furniture and funny bric-a-brac, family pictures hanging at crazy angles on the walls along with huge colorful posters from old airshows. I asked her about that.

"My first husband was a barnstormer," she said. "You know, a stunt pilot. I was always afraid he'd go in a plane crash and wouldn't you know, he fell dead while he was *shaving*! Heart failure."

So she didn't poison him, I surmised vaguely as I looked at trees growing in pots—real *trees* inside a house! And there was a live parrot, green as emerald, that roosted in the trees instead of in a cage. It spoke to me, but I couldn't understand what it was saying. It certainly didn't say Polly wants a cracker. Maybe *Latin*? I turned around and came face to face with a stuffed crow on a mantelpiece. My head jerked back involuntarily and Miss Eddie Mack laughed.

"It can't bite you," she said.

I remembered the dead crow in the cemetery and wondered darkly if it was she who had put it there.

20

Next she led me out back and showed me her green-house. It was hidden and secluded and private, a little enclave of encompassed fertility. It had glass sides and a sloping glass roof fitted into wooden frames. Why was she showing me these things?

"Built it myself," she said, proudly displaying a kind of vaporizer or steam-maker, which she explained kept her plants warm and moist in the winter. "I grow fresh tomatoes year round," she told me.

I had to admit I was intrigued by the way she'd done up the place for herself. There indeed wasn't a domicile like this in all of Yazoo County—or in the entire state of Mississippi, for that matter. Maybe, I thought, she's not as bad as people think.

"How about a cup of herbal tea?" she said.

"Uh, I'm not much on tea, thank you," I said, recalling the two dead husbands in spite of myself. After all, I'd only been around Miss Eddie Mack for five minutes.

"Don't ever be afraid to try somethin' new!" she said. "Come on."

She took me into her kitchen, the most ordinary room in her house. By that I mean that it looked like a regular kitchen. It had a sink and faucets, table and chairs, little red curtains on the windows and a woodburning stove and an oldfashioned icebox with real ice in it. I wondered if Miss Eddie Mack had her ice delivered. Or was the iceman wary of coming here like everybody else?

She lit a Bunsen burner under a water kettle. While she wasn't looking I studied her face. It was wide at the cheekbones, narrow at the temples and had a sharp and angular chin. Straight wrinkles creased her forehead. Her eyes were wideset and she had a way of looking steadily at whatever she was doing. Now, for instance, as she measured out spoonfuls of powdered tea her eyes didn't blink at all. I also noticed that she had big, strong hands—a man's hands—and she picked up things precisely. Some women

21

have nervous hands and are always tapping their fingers. My mother did that. But Miss Eddie Mack had quiet, sure hands.

When the tea kettle began to whistle she turned off the gas burner and poured water into the cups and stirred them with a spoon.

"It's hot," she said, handing me a cup balanced on a saucer. "Blow on it."

I held the cup and saucer as carefully as I could. She waited to see how I'd like her tea, so I puckered my lips and took a tiny sip. I was surprised at the taste, sweet and smooth. This didn't taste like any tea I'd ever had. It was almost too hot to drink, but I blew on it and took another sip. Over the rim of my cup I saw Miss Eddie Mack smile ever so briefly.

If you ever imagined what an elf or a leprechaun might smile like, that's how she smiled. One corner of her mouth dipped downward for an instant and then became a straight line again.

"The Chinese call it Lotus Blossom tea," she said.

I took another swallow and a warm feeling radiated through my body, and for the first time I felt relaxed in her presence.

"It's soporific," she said.

"Sopor-*what*?" I wondered whether this meant Lotus Blossom tea could change a person's shape or transport him somehow into another dreamy dimension.

"Makes you drowsy," she explained. "But only for a moment. Come on, I'll show you around some more. Bring your cup with you, if you like."

She showed me her toolshed. There were all kinds of spades and trowels, rakes and pruning shears and saw-toothed scissors. Everything was hanging neatly on hooks on the wall. She had a work bench with a power saw, and a full set of mechanic's wrenches and pliers. There were tubes of grease and solvent and rubber cement, and rolls

22

of tape of all kinds. In the corner something large was covered with a tarpaulin.

"I like to fix things," she said. "Need a lot of tools." She gave me a look of diffident pride, then led me back into the kitchen and we sat down.

Having completed the tour of the house, I was momentarily at a loss for words. I sipped my tea and tried to think of something to say. I didn't mean to say what I did. It just slipped out.

"Aren't you scared, living up here next door to the cemetery?"

She surprised me with another of those unexpected downturned grins. "There's no more peaceful place than a cemetery."

"Aren't you afraid of ghosts?"

"They don't bother anybody."

"You mean, you *believe* in ghosts!"

"A boy your age has no business talking about ghosts."

"Have you ever seen one? Really, I want to know." I started to take another sip of tea, then noticed her staring straight at me with a sudden hard intensity.

"You had something to do with painting that sign on the Clark Mansion, didn't you?" she said.

I swallowed wrong and started to cough. She reached over and slapped me vigorously on the back.

"It's none of my business," she said. "You don't have to tell me if you don't want to."

I scrupulously set the cup down. "Who said I did that?"

"Nobody. I just had a feeling."

"Do you get feelings like that very often?" I asked in bewilderment.

She rose and went to the sink and started clearing things away. Then she stopped and looked at me over her shoulder.

"Don't pay any attention to those stories people tell about me," she said. "I know you've heard them, about me

23

being the reincarnation of my great-grandmother. Well, all that happened so long ago nobody knows what kind of person she was. Sometimes a town will turn on somebody who's different from everybody else. But the best people resist superstition and fear and think for themselves. You're like that, Willie, or you wouldn't have come to my house in the first place."

She turned back to the sink and gave me a moment to think about what she'd said.

"Do you believe in witches?" I said hesitantly.

She looked out the window. I caught a glimpse of movement and saw that another crow was perched in the bottle tree.

"Like I said, a boy your age has no business asking about witches and ghosts. Take my advice, Willie, and keep your imagination in check."

I didn't know what to say to that. An uncomfortable silence fell between us. I realized I was drumming my fingers on the table, the way my mother did.

"I better be getting home," I said, and stood up. Miss Eddie Mack remained at the sink. "Thanks for the tea," I said. She still didn't say anything. I turned as if to go, then blurted, " *Was she a witch* ?"

"Who?" Miss Eddie Mack said.

"Your great-grandmother."

"What do *you* think?"

"Well, they say..." I began.

"Do you believe everything people say?" she said irritably. "Does it seem reasonable to you that a body could rise up and break chains over a grave?"

"No, ma'am, but..."

"*Think*, Willie, don't just feel. *Think*. Think for yourself."

I considered this for a moment, then said, "She was your great-grandmother?"

"That's right."

"And people thought she was a witch."

24

"Yes?"

"Well, what reason did they have?"

Miss Eddie Mack tightened her lips—was it to keep from smiling?—and said, "My great-grandmother wasn't afraid to live the way she wanted to. People began to talk. By their lights she was peculiar—kept to herself, dressed funny, had strange pets and plants, grew herbs, same as I do. Some of the seeds I started off with, by the way, were given to me by my grandmother, who'd gotten them from her mother. The important thing about my great-grandmother, I reckon, is that she was true to herself, regardless of the consequences. Now me, I don't care what people say. I'm at peace here." She pointed to her heart. "I don't lose a minute's sleep over what people say."

I couldn't help grinning a little—she was so sincere she was almost frowning.

"Well, thanks for talking with me," I said. "And thanks for the tea."

"You're welcome." She turned back to what she was doing. "Come back anytime you like, young man."

She was filling a jar with tap water and didn't look around as I left the house. When I went through her yard the crow flew out of the bottle tree, like any normal crow would. I looked back at Miss Eddie Mack's kitchen window and thought I saw her smiling at me, a soft benign smile I didn't comprehend.

Four

RIVERS APPLEWHITE WAS THE prettiest girl in Mississippi. She had green eyes and brown hair and a smile like nobody else I ever saw. She smelled of trees and clover and sunshine and grass, and she'd laugh with me or be serious just when I needed her to be. I don't know why, but she knew what I was feeling before I knew, myself. She was just about the best girl in the world. Remember how brave she was that night at the Clark Mansion? I'd just caught up with her. For the first time we were exactly the same height.

As the reader may recall, I told numerous stories about Rivers in *Good Old Boy*. Since the events of that memorable year, I could tell others about her, but two among many will suffice for now.

It was about six months after the episode of the Clark Mansion, an early evening of halcyon October. It was a Friday and we didn't have school the next day–a chilly evening with gusting winds, which made you feel good, and happy to be alive. The war was just recently over, only about six weeks, and we *should've* felt good to be alive, what with all the dead children and people all over the world, the starving neglected children wandering even then around sad destroyed Europe that we'd read and heard about, but I guess we didn't know how really fortunate we were: I mean, just to have a chinaberry fight, and to be in America under a big old moon with food to eat and trusted friends all around, even it they *did* want to kill you with chinaberries. There was a huge harvest moon at the horizon, orange and gleaming and bigger it seemed than the world itself. We'd planned the chinaberry fight around my house on Grand Avenue–Bubba, Henjie, Billy, Spit and some others. In a chinaberry combat you need slingshots, tight long rubber bands attached to the wooden, Y-shaped base. Our next door neighbor had the largest chinaberry tree in town. We picked the chinaberries from the tree and put them in a cardboard box before dividing them up. These chinaberries were hard, and as round as marbles, and when they hit you on the skin from a proper slingshot they really hurt. They stung worse than a bee, and made puffy little blisters on the skin. In a chinaberry fight, when a berry from an opponent struck you, according to the rules and regulations of that day long ago, you were dead, and presumably exempt from the fray.

We chose sides (I picked Rivers first), dug our individual supply of chinaberries from the box, and in the invigorating autumn's moonglow went our separate ways. In less than ten minutes I crept up to Henjie in the back alley and killed him with a chinaberry to the left nostril. He moaned and died. Then I snuck into the deep shrubs at the side of my neighbor's house, lay quietly on my back, and waited to ambush Bubba and Billy. I held my breath in anticipation.

I'd been in my secret spot not very long when I looked up. I saw something which curdled my deepest blood.

Just above me, only two or three feet away, was a gigantic spider's web. Even in the shrubbery it glistened in the ghostly moonlight. The web was thick and tangled, and in the middle of it was the biggest, meanest spider I ever saw. It was about the size of my clenched fist, with evil yellow stripes and tangerine coronets and a fiery green crown and dangerous black dots on a pulsating body the color of that night's moon. It was weaving back and forth in its great sinewy web. It seemed to be *writing* something in its own web! This was the "writing spider" of the breed my grandfather Percy had told me about, which weaved the name of its sorry victim before hypnotizing and then assaulting him with its deadly Delta poison. Even now, with its skinny ebony legs and quivering green antennae and thousand surreptitious eyes, it had seen me prone and helpless on the earth beneath it. It was slowly descending toward me. Its venomous descent mesmerized me. I couldn't move or speak. I was paralyzed.

All around me I heard the shouts of my comrades being killed by chinaberries. I lay there breathless and suspended. The gigantic, hideous spider circled down in its horrible silken web. I lost all trace of time. Long moments must've passed. A half hour? An hour? Both sides in the fight were surely long since dead; the game was over. I heard voices from far away: "Where's Willie?"

The spider was at the base of its web examining me. I could almost smell its pungent odor. My throat was choked with thick, cottony saliva, the saliva of abject fear. Then, from just outside the shrubs, came two distinct and friendly whispers. It was my grandfather Percy–and Rivers.

"He's around here somewhere," Percy said.

"Oh! There he is!" Rivers said. She later said she saw my feet protruding in the fallen leaves. "The writing spider!" she shrieked.

I felt their hands on my desperate ankles. Percy and Rivers pulled me right out of there, just as the spider was about to leap onto my face. A long strand of web dangled from my nose, and I sneezed. Percy laughed. "A close call!" he exclaimed. But Rivers bent down and hugged me for a momentary second. She'd never done that before. "Oh, Willie, you even get into trouble with *spiders* ."

After the "writing spider," the second thing I remember the most about Rivers in that October had to do with Old Skip, who really got sick one night, as sick as he ever was. He'd grown tired in our interminable journeyings around the town, and he also must've gotten hold of something bad, some stricken water somewhere, some rotten food maybe. Whatever it was, he looked awful. He was so sick his hair was on end. His nose was dry as dust, and so were his paws. I was scared about Skip.

I lay in the grass with him near the back door of my house. I felt his stomach. It was hot and feverish. Also, little strands of warm saliva were dripping down his mouth, bubbling as they flowed. Mama and Daddy and my grand-daddy Percy came out on the back porch for a second to look, then disappeared inside again, as if they wished to leave Skip and me alone.

I hugged him, then said, "Wait, Skip ." I went inside and brought back a bottle of aspirin and a wet towel. "Don't die."

All of a sudden Rivers appeared with Percy. I suspect now Percy had telephoned her to come. I never wanted to see two people more in my life than Rivers and Percy. Old Skip was shaking all over now. I put my knees astraddle him, and Rivers did, too. I tried to force his mouth open. Rivers and Percy helped me. We put two aspirin under his tongue. He gagged. Then we applied the cool, wet towel to his face. Rivers and I held onto him until he rolled over into the thick weeds and briars bordering the lawn. The briars scratched my arms and made me bleed. I closed Skip's mouth, making him swallow deeply.

29

"It's okay now," Percy said. "I'll leave you."

Skip turned and looked up at Rivers and me. He yawned, then weakly licked my nose, and Rivers' too. His black eyes gleamed in the diaphonous autumn night. He gradually fell asleep. Rivers and I just lay next to him in the grass, the three of us together there. We were tired, too. Rivers tended the little streams of blood on my arms. "Look at all the stars, Willie."

We stayed there for a moment, Skip resting between us, gazing up at the skies. "Thanks, Rivers." Little drops of my blood were on her fingers, not much, but she held her hands before her and looked at the blood, as if thinking.

Then Mama came out. "I'll drive you home, Rivers." And she did. Old Skip was fine the next day, not at all angry about the medicine as far as I could tell, and healthy as a heathen.

Now, on this Monday morning of the new spring six months later, Skip and I were waiting to walk with Rivers to school. She came up to us on the sidewalk and said, "What are you up to, Willie?"

"What do you mean?"

"I don't know, you've got that look."

"What look?" I said.

We began walking up Grand Avenue. The great budding trees were like silhouettes of green, and the earth hummed with movement and surging life, and the very air was filled with leafy strands and the odors of beginning, everything sort of sad and beguiling. Old Skip trotted along between us. A yellow schoolbus drove by, and a girl stuck her head out the window and yelled, "*Hey, Rivers!*"

Rivers waved at her, then said to me, "The look you get sometimes. I know that look. Did you hear about the crow somebody put in the goldfish pool downtown? And the sign?"

"Yeah."

"You didn't have anything to do with that, did you?" She was as earnest as I'd ever seen her. Her green eyes weren't even twinkling.

"Cross my heart and hope to die," I said, feeling in the instant so guilty and remorseful I swiftly changed the subject. "Are you going to the Prom?"

"Of course," she said.

Everybody was talking about the Yazoo High Prom. We were only in the seventh grade, but anybody at the school was allowed to go to the Prom, and almost everybody did. We seventh-graders hadn't started "dating," officially, but there were class picnics and fellowship retreats at Blue Lake (so named, we thought, because the water was so cold it turned us blue in thirty seconds), and hay rides and birthday parties at the skating rink. I guess we were getting used to the idea of dating a little at a time. It was a big step and nobody—at least nobody in the seventh grade—wanted to rush into it. There were no rules, and it was kind of embarrassing.

"Who are you going with?" I said. When Rivers didn't immediately reply, I had the sour, brackish feeling that somebody else had asked her.

I had procrastinated about inviting her, thinking maybe we could just meet at the Country Club where the dance was being held instead of going there together. That way, none of the older boys would see my mother driving us to the dance. It hadn't occurred to me that Rivers might go with somebody else. Rivers with somebody else?

"Oh, somebody," she said.

"*Who!*"

"A good old boy."

"*Who is it!*"

"I'll tell you when he asks me."

"I thought you were going with me!" I exclaimed.

"Well, you haven't asked me."

"*Will-you-go-with-me-then?*" I burst out.

31

"Yes, Willie, I'd love to," she said, as matter-of-factly as anything could be.

We walked on in silence. Rivers was the only girl I could ever do that with, just be quiet, and not feel too uncomfortable about it. We watched the cars turning into the school drive and lining up behind the buses. When we came to the last street corner before the school, Skip turned around the way he always did, without so much as a wag of his tail, and automatically headed home to wait for me to get out of school. At 3:05 he would be waiting on this spot–I mean, on this very crack in the sidewalk–to meet me. We'd walk home and make mayonnaise sandwiches if there wasn't anything else in the refrigerator and then go find a baseball or basketball game somewhere.

"Goodbye, Skip!" Rivers called.

When we got to school, the students were lounging about outside. Rivers and I split up as usual. She started talking to a group of twittery girls, and I went over to where Bubba, Billy and Henjie were, in the dappled shade of a giant oak.

"Everybody's talking about the witches' signs!" Bubba said, his eyes bright with excitement.

"Keep your voice down," I said, drawing them in around me. "We got to make a secret pact."

"What for?" Henjie said.

"To make sure nobody tells," Bubba said. "Ain't that right, Willie?"

"What's to tell?" Henjie said. "We played a joke and that's the end of it."

"Is it?" I said. They all looked at me.

Henjie shook his head. "Uh-uh, Willie. Oh, no. Count me out."

"Coward!" Bubba taunted. Henjie grabbed him and they wrestled a little with each other, plopping around on the lush thick grass.

32

"Okay, okay, break it up," I said. "What I mean is, there may be more to this than meets the eye."

"Like what?" Billy said.

"There may be witches and devil worshippers sure 'nuff in Yazoo," I said, "and it behooves us to find out exactly what we're dealing with."

"*Behooves!*" Bubba said. "That's pretty high-falutin', Willie."

"Well, suit yourself," I said. "I'm going to the library after school to see if they have any books about witchcraft."

"The *library!*" Now it was Billy's turn to complain. "You mean, waste a perfectly good afternoon looking at *books*?"

The first bell rang for homeroom, and everybody began drifting inside the building.

"You don't have to go if you don't want to," I said, and went into the school.

The Yazoo library stood on a gentle triangular lot formed by the intersection of Washington and Main Streets. It always seemed cool even on the hottest days. This had something to do with the serene, unhurried atmosphere, the way your body slowed down and your mind took over. I could sit in one of the big, soft chairs with *Huckleberry Finn* or *Kidnapped* or *Treasure Island* or *The Call of the Wild* and forget about everything else.

My comrades, however, didn't seem to share this enthusiasm. They reluctantly followed me into the public library that afternoon when school was out.

"Where do we find a book on witches?" Billy whispered, looking suspiciously at the rows of book shelves all around us.

"Let's start in the card catalogue," I said.

"That's just what I was gonna suggest," Henjie said.

I thumbed through the catalog and discovered the Yazoo library had only one book on witches.

"Listen to this," I said. "The title is *Witches and Goblins*."

"Oh, boy!" Bubba said.

33

"Now you're cooking with gas," Billy said.

But Mrs. Leone Martin, the librarian, informed us that the book was checked out and that she'd already had twelve calls for it.

"Who's got it?" I said.

"I can't give out that information, Willie. You'll have to wait your turn. With all the scare, everybody wants to know about witches these days. People are worried."

"Well, we tried," Bubba said. "Now let's go get a Dr. Pepper and some peanuts."

"Wait a minute," I said, and motioned them to come around a bookshelf where Mrs. Martin couldn't see us. "Billy, why don't you ask her to help you find the latest Nancy Drew mystery or something."

"Nancy Drew!" he exclaimed. "That's for *girls*."

"Well, the Hardy Boys, then. Anything to get her away from her desk and give me time to see who's checked out *Witches and Goblins*."

Just saying the words gave me a tender thrill. I remember them to this day. I silently repeated them to myself and noticed Bubba and Billy doing the same: *Witches and Goblins*. It had a ring to it.

While Billy distracted Mrs. Martin by helping him find a book, I slipped around her desk, pulled out the drawer where she kept the check-out file and went through it until I came to the *Witches and Goblins* card, which had only been checked out three times in the history of the library. It read:

> *Witches and Goblins*
> Sept. 14, 1938 - E. McBride
> Feb. 3, 1942 - E. McBride
> April 2, 1946 - A. Abbott

I heard Mrs. Martin coming back and quickly closed the drawer, then feigned to be perusing the magazine rack near her desk. She was telling Billy how glad she was that he had at last become interested in reading. Billy mumbled that he was glad she was glad.

We waited while Billy checked out a Hardy Boys mystery, then we crowded out the front entrance.

"Guess who!" I said when we were outside.

"I give up!" Bubba said.

"Miss Abbott, that's who."

"What does *she* want with a book about witches?" Bubba said.

"Maybe she's a witch!" Henjie said.

"Nah," Billy spoke up. "She just has to know everything about everything."

"Well, that's that," Bubba said. "We'll have to wait till she brings the book back."

"Maybe not," I said. "Miss Abbott borrowed the book from the library. We can borrow the book from Miss Abbott."

"You mean, go in her house and take it!" Henjie was horrified.

"Why not?" I felt somehow light and airy, free as a bird in flight. My friends stood in front of the library staring at me up and down as if I *were* some kind of odd jungle bird with a long beak and bright red and blue feathers.

"What're you talkin' about, Willie?" Bubba said.

"I'm talkin' about borrowin' a book. We'll take it back when we're through with it. If we read fast, we can get it back before she notices it's missing."

"You're talking about breaking into her *house*?" Henjie said. "Uh-uh, Willie, forget it. There's a name for that. We'll end up in Parchman Penal Farm." As usual when he was taken aback by human circumstances, Henjie burped.

"Okay," I said. "See you later."

I started walking up the sidewalk, whistling carelessly to myself. Billy and Bubba rushed after me. Henjie lingered behind, kicking self-consciously at sticks and clods of dirt here and there. Billy was staring at the Hardy Boys novel in his hand as if to say, He got me to check out this silly book for nothing.

A minute later all three of them caught up with me. It didn't take much persuading to get them to go along with the plan. The funny thing about it was that I seemed to be two persons at once. One side of me did the talking while the other hovered about ten feet off the ground, watching and listening. It was a weird feeling but I didn't stop to think about it or to try to explain it to myself. I had no idea why I was that way.

We went up a winding little alley that came out by Miss Abbott's house. The whole town was abundant with alleys like this, little isolated pathways inherited from an earlier day amidst the bustling human commerce, running with scant design or reason in their wonderful timelessness behind the houses and stores and barns and chickenyards and gardens. Even in 1946 you could get away with anything in those alleys. Henjie stayed at one end of this alley as a lookout while Billy went to the other.

"If something happens," I told them, "split up and meet at the treehouse."

This was a kind of clubhouse we'd built out of scrap lumber in a towering red oak tree across the railroad tracks on the outskirts of town. Our previous headquarters had been the chickenshed in Henjie's back yard, but Henjie's father had torn it down when he stopped raising chickens.

Bubba and I went into the vacant lot behind Miss Abbott's house. It was densely overgrown with blackberry bushes and honeysuckle vines and pink dogwood and blackgum trees and great patches of the new clover and Johnson grass. We pretended to be playing, searching languidly for birds' nests or rabbit hutches or ant hills, then dropped down out of sight and crawled on our bellies to a fence bordering Miss Abbott's property. The wire fence was rusty and loose, and we crept under it and kept behind a row of azalea and camelia shrubs until we reached the rear of the house. Her car was gone, so we concluded nobody was inside.

I tried the back door. It was locked. We went around to the garage and tried the inside door. It too was locked.

"I wonder where she keeps her key," I said. Bubba looked under the mat but found nothing. I ran my hand along the top of the door frame and lo and behold there the key was. I inserted it in the lock and turned it. There was a click, and I opened the door.

"I don't feel so hot about this," Bubba said.

"You want to wait here then?" I said.

"Somebody needs to keep a lookout," he said, not looking me in the eye, adding, "Just in case."

"Yeah, just in case," I said. "I'll be back in a minute."

I played with the doorknob, deciding how the door could be locked automatically by pushing a button and shutting it.

"Why are you doing that?" Bubba said.

"Because if Miss Abbott shows up and we have to run for it, she'll expect this door to be locked."

"Oh, yeah. –Do you think she'll show up!"

"You never know. We have to be prepared. Holler if you see her coming, and then get out of here quick. Put this key back where we got it."

"What will *you* do if she comes?"

"I'll go out the other back door and lock it behind me, same as this one. Hey, we're wasting time. I'm going to get the book."

I tip-toed through the kitchen, so clean and white and antiseptic it could have been a hospital operating room. It even smelled faintly of ammonia. In the dining room the table and sideboard gleamed with furniture polish. The living room was also exceptionally neat, yet crammed with figurines of waltzing princes and princesses, framed teacher awards on the wall, paintings of meadowed arcadias and statuettes of famous-looking men. There was a

37

spinet piano in the corner and overstuffed Victorian chairs with lace doilies on the arms. They looked like they were expecting company. The whole house, in fact, seemed to stand at rigid attention like a classroom of students dreading a surprise examination.

I couldn't help comparing this house with Miss Eddie Mack's. It had never occurred to me how a house reminds you of its owner. I guess I'd never been in a grownup's house all by myself before—especially uninvited and on a dubious mission. Both Miss Eddie Mack's and Miss Abbott's homes were cluttered with old lady paraphernalia, but there at least seemed to be some *purpose* in the plants and trees and pictures and utensils that Miss Eddie Mack kept for herself. As precise and exact as Miss Abbott's house was, I couldn't help feeling that something was not right in it. The "Witch's" house seemed open to experience, to *possibilities*, yet this house seemed only to guard against them. Those lace doilies seemed to say, Watch out! Don't get this chair dirty.

I noticed some books and papers stacked neatly on a desk in the parlor adjoining the living room. Miss Abbott had brought some papers home to grade. I remembered those tests when I was in her fourth grade class. What agony they'd been! You not only had to answer word for word what Miss Abbott had taught you, but your spelling had to be perfect, and even your handwriting. She wanted those loops and swirls to be evenly rounded, the I's dotted just right, the T's crossed three-fourths of the way up. Whew! I thought to myself. How did I ever get out of the fourth grade? How did I ever escape Miss Abbott?

I found the library book, *Witchcraft and Goblins*, under the stack of papers. Just holding it in my hand gave me a small ecstasy, as a pirate might feel on finding a chest of buried treasure long retrieved from the darkest breast of the sea. I was about to open it and see if there were any pictures of witches and goblins when I heard Bubba yell, *"Willie, car coming!"*

My mind was amazingly lucid and calm. Isn't it curious how vivid things are in a moment like this? I carefully arranged the stack of books and papers as I'd found them—though without the library book—then I walked down a hall to the back of that spotless, perfect dwelling. My principal concern was not whether I'd get away unseen but that Miss Abbott might sight Bubba as she drove her car into her garage. The rear door was at the end of the hall. It also had a button that made it lock automatically when I closed it behind me. As I crept outside and shut the door behind me, I heard a car door slam inside the garage. I made my way around the corner of the house and crawled behind the row of azaleas again until I reached the fence at the back of the lot.

Bubba was lying in the weeds just on the other side of the fence. He held up the wire while I wriggled under it.

"Did you get it?" he said. His eyes were so big the whites showed all around the irises, the way they did when anything interested him.

"Yeah." I held out the book. "Did she see you?"

"No, let's *go!*"

Henjie and Billy were awaiting us at the end of the alley. They were worried that we'd taken so long, but when they acknowledged that we'd gotten away clean they gradually calmed down. I also suggested to them that we weren't doing anything too bad as long as we put the book back where we got it.

"Put it under your shirt!" Billy said. I stuck the book under the waistband of my bluejeans in the back.

"Why not just leave it in the library book-drop when we're through with it?" Bubba said, as we walked up the sidewalk trying not to look seditious.

"Because the librarian knows we asked for the book!" Henjie said.

"That's right," I said. "The best thing would be if we could put it back before Miss Abbott notices it's missing."

"But how will you get into her house with her in it?" Bubba said.

"I'll put it in her car," I said. "She'll think she left it there."

"Miss Abbott?" Bubba said. "She never forgets anything."

"There's always a first time," I said.

Five

THE WOODS ON THE other side of the railroad tracks had never looked so dark and inviting. Back then the woods came right up to the town, to its streets and boulevards and yards, before they cut down the woods and paved them over. Why would anybody want to destroy these fine old woods? Nobody visited this place much, which was why we'd built our treehouse here. The gullies and ridges and declivities were covered with trees and brush, and rotting leaves of our vanished November were piled two feet deep on the ground, and there was a patina of both death and growth all around it. The only noises were the vibrant birdcalls and the rustle of our own stealthy footsteps.

It was raining a little now, a hesitant rain under suddenly tense heavens. Beneath the brassy skies the earth and trees were incredibly deep and green, and from the river came the melancholy echo of a boat's horn. It was a sly and silent town then, and it was easy to absorb its every rhythm and heartbeat, and the slightest sound from far

41

away. I loved those funny silences. One by one we climbed into our treehouse, which was nothing but a modest plank floor nailed across two arbitrary limbs. Overhead was a roof made of fading branches. Bubba opened a pack of Life-savers and passed them around. I sucked on a mint and started reading about witches and devils.

"Are there any pictures?" Billy asked.

"Read it out loud, Willie," Bubba said. "We're ready."

So I read how witchcraft got started in ancient Egypt and continued into the times of the Roman Empire and the Middle Ages. Superstitious people divided the world into kingdoms of good and evil. A benevolent god ruled in the daytime, while the Devil, or god of darkness, ruled at night. Witches were people who believed in the Devil. Some witches weren't evil, however, but sought the gift of prophecy so they could help mankind survive natural ca-tastrophes such as storms or pestilence or fire or ice. Some people paid witches to cast spells on their rivals, cursing a competitor's crops or family or making him sick. To obtain power over an individual, the witch first needed some physical part of him. A lock of hair or nail paring would do nicely.

"What's a paring?" Billy interrupted.

"It means *clipping*," Bubba said. "Like when you clip your toe-nails."

"My toe-nails don't need clipping," Billy said.

"Everybody's does," Bubba said.

"Listen to this," I said, and continued reading:

To lay a curse, the witch muttered the victim's name over and over while burning his hair or a piece of his cloth-ing. Some people were so afraid of witches' curses that they used false names all their lives.

"Wow!" Bubba said.

"But if that was what everybody called them," Henjie reasoned, "wouldn't that eventually get to be their real name?"

42

"Never mind," I said.

Witches were thought to have devil marks, which could include moles or birthmarks that resembled toads or horned creatures such as goats. A test that determined if a woman was a witch was finding a spot on the skin where a pin could be stuck without causing pain. Such a spot was said to be where the devil had touched the woman.

"Boy, that test would *hurt!*" Bubba said. "Look, is this a mole on my arm?"

"Here's a splinter," Billy said. "Stick that mole and see if you're a witch." We watched Bubba stick himself.

"Ouch, that hurts!" Bubba said.

"The pin test was better than the water test," I said. "Witches were supposed to be able to float on water. They threw a suspected witch into a pond and if she floated, they burned her at the stake. If she drowned, she wasn't a witch."

"She didn't get much out of it, did she?" Billy said. "Don't sound like a particularly good deal to me."

"Reckon Miss Eddie Mack can swim?" Bubba said, half-joking.

"She's no witch!" I said defensively.

"How do you know?" Billy said.

"Because I went to see her," I replied. "I've been in her house."

"You did!" they cried together.

I told them about going to her house that afternoon, how she caught me peeking through her privet hedge and took me inside. They wanted to know all about what the place looked like. They were impressed that I'd been there, all except Billy, who had become engrossed with a mole on his arm.

"What's this mole look like to you?" Billy asked Henjie.

"A chicken," Henjie said.

"I ain't no *chicken!*" Billy cried, and began wrestling with Henjie.

43

"Look out," Bubba said. "Somebody's gonna fall off." He passed the mints around again.

"I don't think you have a devil mark," I told Billy. "There aren't any horns on your mole."

"But it really does look like a chicken," Bubba said, and ducked when Billy took a perfunctory swipe at him.

"I may be little but I ain't chicken!" Billy muttered to himself.

I resumed reading aloud about how devil dances were a big part of the religion of certain African, South American and Tibetan tribes. Devil worshippers believed that the powers of evil were as great as the powers of good. They believed their combined evil intentions could cause harm to their enemies.

"Does that mean whoever in Yazoo is making those devil signs wants to *hurt* somebody?" Bubba said. "Who's doin' all this, anyway?"

"*We* made the star in a circle," Billy reminded him, "and we didn't mean to hurt nobody."

"Yeah, but we was just foolin' around," Bubba said. "Didn't have nothin' better to do. And, besides, if Spit hadn't told us how to make it, we wouldn't've known about it."

"Let's make a secret pact," I said.

"What?" Bubba said.

"Let's form our own brotherhood," I continued. "It tells you how, right here in this book. We've got to fight fire with fire, don't we?"

"Yeah!" Billy said. "Let's fight fire with fire. –Uh, who are we fightin', Willie?"

"Willie don't know," Bubba said.

"If we follow the directions in that book," Henjie said thoughtfully, "wouldn't that make *us* witches?"

"Only women can be witches," I said. "They call male witches 'warlocks.' "

"Warlocks," Billy echoed, "that sounds like Indians."

44

"Warlocks," Bubba and Henjie repeated solemnly.

"We'd only be *temporary* warlocks," I said. "And since it's for a good cause, we couldn't be *bad* warlocks."

"Do you get to be a warlock by reading in a book?" Bubba said doubtfully.

"It's not what you read," I explained, "but what you believe. If you believe you have the power, then you do."

I didn't know if this was true but it seemed to make sense.

"Okay," Bubba agreed. "What do we have to do?"

"Basically," I said, "you sign your name in blood." I'd also read this in *Tom Sawyer*, although this was the Twentieth Century. How do you beat Tom Sawyer? At least he'd been dead and gone for many years.

There was a silence, then Henjie said, "Your full name, or will your first name do?"

"Seein' as how we're only going to be temporary warlocks," I said, "I reckon we can get by with an 'X,' the way people do who don't know how to write. That's legal."

"Is this gonna be *legal*?" Henjie said.

"Of course not," Bubba put in. "This is just between us."

"And the devil," Henjie said.

We got pretty quiet for a minute, looking each other over. Then I said, "Let's leave the devil out of it."

This seemed to pacify everybody, and we emptied our pockets looking for paper. The only scrap among us was Bubba's Lifesaver wrapper. He gingerly unwrapped the rest of the candy and gave us two pieces each, then smoothed the paper flat on the rough wooden planks. We compared pocket knives to see whose blade was the sharpest. Then we found a little twig to use as a "pen" to write with. We were ready except for having some proper words to say in the spirit of profound and most reverential ceremony. Everybody looked at me.

"There isn't anything in the book that tells you exactly how to do it," I said. "I reckon it will be okay if we say, 'We

45

hereby declare ourselves to be temporary warlocks and promise on peril of our lives...' "

"What does *that* mean?" Billy said.

"That sounds kind of strong, Willie," Bubba said.

"Yeah," Henjie agreed. "That's goin' too far."

"Okay, let's leave out the peril part," I said. "Just declare yourself to be a temporary warlock and sign your X. Who's goin' first?"

Billy suggested we do it by size, which meant Bubba had to go first. We watched him pause, then meticulously stick a tiny little hole in his left thumb and squeeze out a drop of blood.

"Did that hurt?" Henjie said.

"Not too bad," Bubba said. "Could've been worse." He dipped the twig in his blood and wrote an X, while I held the paper down. He smiled, wan and triumphant.

Each of us followed. Then we sat back and looked at the Lifesaver wrapper with the four X's on it. I don't know why, but it seemed like we'd done something big, something tremendous and inexorable. We sat there grinning at each other like four cats over a bowl of cream. There was no need to say anything.

We just sat wordlessly in our treehouse encompassed in the moist green shadows and the buoyant Yazoo earth. Perched twelve feet above the ground in our hidden glade, we felt practically *invincible*. Fools that we were.

Six

ON TUESDAY AFTERNOON MRS. Posey, our Social Studies teacher, a debilitating lady and thin as a wisp, was about to hand out midterm tests when a voice crackled through the loudspeaker on the wall. It was a pronouncement from Mr. Barnes, our principal.

"Students, ahhhh," Mr. Barnes began, "I would like to, ahhhhh, inform you that an assembly will be held in the auditorium." The loudspeaker system clicked as Mr. Barnes turned it off, then it clicked back on with a nervous burst of stacatto. "Ahhhhh, immediately," he added.

I glanced at Bubba, who sat across the row from me in the Social Studies class. I caught his eye and nodded at him. He looked down at his notebook in cool apprehension. We could guess why this assembly was being summoned. "My goodness, couldn't this have been announced sooner!" Mrs. Posey complained as she locked her test papers in her desk.

All the students were talking at once, an infectious chorus of speculation, as we crowded the hallway and filed into the auditorium. It was like a holiday. Nobody could remember when Mr. Barnes had called an assembly without announcing it a day or more ahead of time. Henjie and Billy met Bubba and me outside the auditorium. Henjie looked so guilty and Billy so sorry and shifty-eyed that I knew we couldn't sit together.

"Split up," I said. "And *don't* go around looking like criminals!"

I saw Rivers sitting near the back row. She pointed to an empty seat next to her. I didn't mind that mostly girls were sitting on this row. In fact, that suited me perfectly under the circumstances. I went down the row and slid into the seat.

"What's this assembly for?" Rivers said excitedly.

"I don't know," I said, glancing around so she couldn't look me in the eye, knowing me as she did.

"Well, whatever it is," she went on, "it got me out of having to recite the opening lines of *The Ancient Mariner* in English class."

I recited:

> *It is an ancient Mariner,*
> *And he stoppeth one of three,*
> *'By thy long gray beard and glittering eye,*
> *Now wherefore stopp'st thou me?'* "

"Oh, Willie!" she said. "Why's it so easy for you? It's not fair."

Several chairs were arranged on the stage behind the speaker's podium. Three men walked on with Principal Barnes and took their seats: Father O'Hara, Reverend Turnipseed of the First Baptist Church, and the Yazoo High football coach, "Red" Foley. Mr. Barnes went to the podium and opened the assembly by calling on the student body president to lead us in the Pledge of Allegiance. Then Mr. Barnes took over.

"This assembly has been called, ah, students because of

a situation that is...developing. There have been a number of calls from concerned parents. So we would like to clear the, ah, air, and get on with our business. As you may or may not know, this incident of the dead blackbird being hoisted on the flagpole..."

The student body president whispered something to Mr. Barnes, who bent over to listen, then addressed the assembly again.

"...ah, dead crow, I should say—is just one of several recent incidents of someone defacing public property."

I thought, *What a great country this is, where you can get out of midterm tests by harmlessly hoisting a dead crow on a flagpole.*

I'd gone back to the cemetery just at dark, the day before, and retrieved that dead crow off the Witch's grave.

"There's no point in letting it go to waste," I'd told Bubba, Henjie and Billy. I'd phoned them and suggested they meet me in the schoolyard.

"What're you gonna do with it?" Bubba said, glancing around as if the police were coming to arrest him at any minute.

"You mean, what're *we* gonna do?" I said. "Somebody put a crow in the waterworks goldfish pool. Well, we'll go 'em one better. If we start a competition, sooner or later they're bound to overplay their hand and we can flush 'em out into the open, whoever they are."

"Maybe we'll get caught first," Bubba said.

"Think positive," I said, and tied the crow's feet to the chain on the flagpole in front of Yazoo High and ran it up about half-mast.

The sky had grown purple and the first stars were coming out. Venus was so big it could have been right over Belzoni. The courthouse chimes struck eight. The dead crow looked derelict hanging there, so limp and silent and still.

"That'll get somebody's attention," I said.

"What if that crow ain't completely dead?" Billy said.

"It's dead, all right," I said. "This ain't hurting that old crow any."

"If it wasn't dead, it could fly down and *attack* us!" Henjie said. His face looked pale and impetuous in the vanishing amber light.

"Yeah," Billy played along with the notion, "the attack of the Killer Crow!"

"Come on, fellas, get serious," I said.

"I hope that ain't nobody's pet crow," Bubba said.

"Yeah, me too," Billy said.

"Look, probably some owl killed that old crow," I said. "Remember, we signed a pact. We've got a *mission* to do. The witch squad never sleeps. Something's goin' on, and it's not us."

"Witch squad? Hey, Willie, you mean us? Or *them*?" Bubba said, but I was already fading away into the enveloping dark. I stopped and looked back. *Them*? My friends were standing close together, gazing at the crow we'd lifted up together. It *was* eerie, even if we'd created it ourselves. All of a sudden, Billy, Henjie and Bubba started walking away fast. Then Bubba began to trot, and the others too. Soon they broke into a sprint, and the last thing I saw was Billy, who was the fastest, beginning to pull away from them. I started to laugh, but then I heard the metal tabs on the chain clinking against the flagpole.

The crow seemed to be moving.

Part of me said, It's just the wind, and part of me said, Get out of here, and What are you doing?

"We've been getting calls from concerned parents," Mr. Barnes was speaking again, "about this situation regarding certain signs of, ah, witchcraft and such nonsense that've been found. The dead crow was removed by our janitor Robert before he raised the flag this morning. Now I personally don't think that anyone of you would do such a thing."

50

A buzzing excitement ran through the student body like a mighty electric current, snapping and popping as it went. I could've leapt onto the stage and shaken Mr. Barnes's hand. Then he introduced Reverend Turnipseed and asked us to pay close attention to what he had to say. Reverend Turnipseed approached the podium.

"The Devil," he said, looking right and left with a broad, penetrating frown, "has been with us for centuries." He paused to let that idea sink in. "We know how to deal with him. That's what Christianity is all about, boys and girls. But let us be clear about something: these are just hoodlums playing sick jokes."

I thought of the crow hanging limp and obsidian against the April stars. Well, we had our reasons, even if we couldn't explain them succinctly just now.

"Let us be concerned, yes," Reverend Turnipseed continued, "but let us not become overly alarmed by these senseless, foolish acts." He paused histrionically and glanced at Father O'Hara, who nodded in agreement. "It's normal," Reverend Turnipseed went on, "for parents to be worried about the safety of their children, but at the same time we must remain calm. Be alert, yes. Be informed, yes. Be aware, yes! But do not run scared. I repeat, do not run scared! We've got the Devil outnumbered. He has no chance against our combined faith. I have every confidence in you. Thank you, boys and...young men and young women. And now I'll turn the meeting over to Father O'Hara."

There was a touch of polite applause, then the students fell attentive as the priest took the podium.

"Thank you, Reverend Turnipseed. I would like to re-iterate that there is no need for panic. I realize that some threatening phonecalls have been made and some animals apparently sacrificed..."

A murmur arose now from the youthful audience. I sat up alertly. Since our crow was already dead, what *sacrifice*

51

was he talking about? Then it occurred to me with the shameful force of revelation that what we had been simulating was actually a witch's sacrifice.

"...but that is no cause for widespread alarm," Father O'Hara went on. He paused for a moment, and as he did I summoned the nerve to raise my hand. A number of the students turned to look at me, when the priest recognized me and called out, "Yes, Willie?"

I stood up. I saw Henjie and Bubba staring at me in stricken surprise.

"Can you tell us about those threatening phonecalls, Father?" I asked.

"Well, I believe..." Father O'Hara hesitated, glancing questioningly at Mr. Barnes, who rose and reluctantly moved to the podium again.

"Certain threats have been made over the phone," he said and immediately returned to his seat. Again I raised my hand.

"Excuse me, Mr. Barnes," I said, "what did the callers say?" I saw Bubba and Henjie frowning warily at me.

"If you *must* know, Willie," he said, glaring at me as if he and I were carrying on a private conversation in this tense and crowded chamber, "someone threatened to sacrifice children to the Devil." He stopped, stifling as if by conscious will whatever else he meant to say, and five hundred students from Yazoo's seventh through the twelfth grades all gasped at the same time.

"We don't put any stock in, ah, such anonymous threats, of course..." Mr. Barnes went on, but by now a collective muttering rose in the audience, obscuring his words. I could hear girls saying *sacrifice* all over the auditorium.

Rivers passed me a note: "Would they really sacrifice little children?" I wrote "No!" on it, and handed it back to her. But I was worried.

When Mr. Barnes finally got everybody quietened down again, he was obviously so frustrated he forgot what he meant to say. He probably hadn't intended to describe the sacrifice threats. But it was good and out, now. He looked around and saw Coach Foley sitting on the edge of his chair, leaning one elbow on his knee as if getting down into a three-point stance.

"Let's hear from Coach Foley," the principal said. "Coach?"

The football players sitting on the front row in their letter jackets whistled and cheered. The coach put his hands in his pockets to demonstrate how serious he was.

"We have us a situation here that, seems to me, is kinda like a ballgame. The Devil's won the toss and is kicking off. The ball's coming to you. I say, let Jesus run interference. Get behind Jesus and he'll roll-block the old Devil out of your way. Like I always say in our team huddle just before kickoff, dedicate this ballgame to Jesus Christ and you'll have clear sailing into the endzone of life!"

When the assembly finally dispersed, everybody was talking in the downstairs hall about human sacrifice and the Devil. As usual the seniors walked back to their classes together, the sophomores and juniors stayed in a gathering pack, while we junior high students went next door to our own building. Because I had spoken up during assembly, naturally I drew some attention.

"They say them devil worshipers practice *lewd* rites," Muttonhead Shepherd said.

"What's lewd?" Billy said.

"Ask Willie," Henjie said. "He claims to know everything."

I knew my friends were irritated with me for speaking out, but before I could reply, Kay, a majorette in the band, grabbed me by the arm and said, "Do you think they'd snatch somebody off the *street*?"

"No, I don't believe they'd take that chance," I said. I saw Henjie, Bubba and Billy standing on the landing as though

to distance themselves from me. They thought I was showing off. Was I?

Margaret, a cheerleader, approached me and asked,
"What's a Black Sabbath?"

"That's when the devil worshipers hold a religious rite,"
I said. "But I can't talk right now, Margaret."

I told Rivers I'd see her later and climbed the stairs to
explain to my friends that I'd asked those questions at assembly so nobody would suspect us of anything. They
looked at me as if they thought I was deranged. As we
started upstairs we overheard two other girls talking on
the steps ahead of us.

"It's all a bunch of hooey, ain't it?" one was saying. "I
mean, there may be some old hobos or bums in the woods
drinking beer and hollering around a campfire, but they
wouldn't sacrifice girls, would they?"

This was the first I had heard about sacrificing *girls*. It
was unbelievable how everybody added to the rumors.

"They practice secret rites out there in the woods," another said.

"They can walk barefoot on burning coals," the first girl
said.

I was reminded of the time our Cub Scout troop went
camping in the Delta and somebody accidentally started a
brush fire. We ran around trying to beat it out with
branches and blankets but just when we thought we had
it contained, it broke out all over again in another spot.
The crackle and swirl of students' voices in the halls had
that same tinderbox aspect. A fire of panic was licking at
Yazoo High. Something strange was happening out there,
something bad and beyond our control, and none of it our
fault, although I was beginning to feel a little sinful and
ashamed. Not even thirteen, with all the earlier successful
hoaxes and then the famous triumph of the Clark Mansion, was I developing what people called "the big head"?
For the first time in my life I wondered if I were being too

54

clever for my own good. Hadn't Miss Eddie Mack said too much imagination was a bad thing? I made myself dismiss such things from my mind. But I was feeling older.

"We gotta talk, Willie," Bubba said, when we reached the second floor.

"Yeah, we gotta be careful now," Henjie added.

"Okay, okay," I said. "But let's don't be seen together on the school grounds. Meet at my house after school and bring your gloves. We can practice shagging fly balls while we decide what to do next."

"Next?" Bubba said as we went back to Social Studies.

Seven

"NORMA'S PET SHOP," a woman answered.

"Do you have any dogs marked down?" I asked in a throaty, Yankee voice.

"Marked down for what?"

"For sacrifice," I said, and hung up the phone.

"Willie, I don't like this," Bubba said, and bit off half a candy bar to accentuate his disaffection.

We were standing around in Bubba's den. Bubba's mother always kept snacks for Bubba and his friends.

"If we're goin' to flush the *real* devil worshippers out," I said, "we have to keep up the pressure."

"But you don't know if there's any real devil worshippers out there!" Henjie said, drowning the chocolate with a hefty gulp of Coke. Then he belched thoughtfully.

"Let's catch flies while we talk it over," I said. "I think better when I'm playing baseball."

We started up the street carrying a bat and a few balls and gloves. The weather had turned warm, and little particles of springtime things floated dreamily in the air, and Old Skip sometimes bit at them with his teeth. There seemed more police cars cruising around town than usual, and old ladies were gathered on street corners whispering. There was a vacant lot on the other side of town where we could usually organize a pickup game with some black boys who always came out and played with us. We only saw them when we played baseball or football or at the Dixie Theatre, where they sat above us in the balcony.

"Betty Lou Pickens was goin' around after school sayin' a virgin's gonna be sacrificed on Good Friday," Bubba said.

"That's day after tomorrow," Henjie said.

"What's a virgin?" Billy said. We all looked at him. "Aw, I *know* that!" he said. "I just forgot for a second."

We were passing Lucky Dan's Pawn Shop on Main Street when Bubba stopped and said, "Isn't that Mr. Barnes's wife? Look, she's buying a *gun.*"

We edged inside and stood at the counter affecting to look at some knives and microscopes and binoculars. Sure enough, the principal's wife was selecting a pistol from several that Lucky Dan, a substantial figure in soiled khakis and a green tractor cap, had laid out in a row on the glass counter.

"The thirty-eight's better for home security, Mrs. Barnes," Lucky Dan was saying.

"This one's so cute, though," she said.

"Yeah, but that twenty-two's kinda light."

"Well, all right," she said.

"Want me to wrap the thirty-eight for you, Mrs. Barnes?" Lucky Dan asked

"Yes, please." She glanced over her shoulder uneasily. "And put in some bullets, if you don't mind."

"How many, a box?"

"Whatever you think's necessary. A dozen will probably do."

After the proprietor had wrapped the pistol in brown

57

parcel paper, Mrs. Barnes paid him, carefully put the package in the bottom of her shopping bag, and departed precipitously without looking behind her. She got in her car and drove off quickly.

"Well, boys," Lucky Dan said, "if you're lookin' for pistols, I'm pretty low on stock. All I've got left is three forty-five Colt automatics and, let's see, this little bitty twenty-two and that thirty-two Beretta over there. Most of the twenty-twos went fast, bein' the cheapest, you know. I still got plenty of rifles."

"Been doin' a lot of business?" I asked casually.

"This's been the greatest day," said Lucky Dan, "in the history of this store. And it's been here since 'thirty-seven."

"What caused it, you reckon?" I said.

"Oh, the devil worshippin', no doubt about it!" he said. "And the sacrifices. People feel the need to protect theirselves." Then he got serious, and added, "Every American citizen has the right to bear arms. It's in the Constitution, ain't it? Well, what can I do for you boys?"

"Nothin', we were just lookin'," I said. We went outside. There was an old man sitting on the bench in front of the shop, reading a paper. He brightened up and looked us over with a quizzical, challenging expression.

"Has that there dawg of yourn got his driver's license yet?" he asked me.

"No sir. At least, if he has, he hasn't told me about it."

"Ha-ha-ha. Well, if he keeps on drivin', I reckon he'll get his license 'fore you get yourn." And he petted Skip on the head.

"Yes sir," I said. "Are you through with that newspaper?"

"It ain't mine," he said, abandoning it carelessly on the bench. "You're welcome to it."

I picked it up and we continued down Main Street while I read the front-page story in the *Yazoo Herald* out loud to the others:

58

VANDALISM BREAKS OUT
CULT ACTIVITY SUSPECTED

In separate incidents this week, a sign was found painted in blood on the old Clark Mansion west of Yazoo, consisting of a star within a circle which is reputed to be a sign of witchcraft. Apparently, the sign was painted Friday night. The sheriff's office reported that the blood used was of animal origin. It is not known whether the prank was the work of practical jokers or demon worshippers. No other evidence of witchcraft was found at the scene.

On Saturday morning a dead crow was found near the city waterworks, along with another strange sign written in blood. Yesterday, another crow was found hoisted on the flagpole at Yazoo High School.

Law enforcement officials do not know if the incidents are connected. Sheriff Biggers urges citizens to remain calm. An investigation is underway.

Accompanying the article was a large photograph of Father O'Hara rubbing out the Latin inscription with his handkerchief: *Venum Daemonus.* "That's two for us and one for them," I said when I'd finished reading.

"What do you mean?" Bubba said. "This ain't no *contest!*"

"What's the matter with you, Willie?" Henjie said.

"Nothing," I said. "Just kiddin'."

"Well, it looks to me like it's gettin' a little more serious than just kiddin' around," he said.

"That's why we made a pact," I said.

"What?" Billy said.

"You know, when we signed the Lifesaver wrapper."

"That's startin' to get old, Willie," Bubba said. "It was fun when we painted the Clark Mansion and stole the book from Miss Abbott..."

"We took that book back," I put in.

"...and even when we signed our X's in blood," he continued. "But it's not like we signed a major league contract or somethin'."

"Yeah!" Henjie agreed.

"Come on," I said. "Let's go hit some flies."

We passed on through the business section of downtown Yazoo, barren and sedate on this day, and went to the vacant lot where we always played. It was an old corn field grown over with grass. Because of its location between the black and white sections of town, it had become a meeting place where boys of different races could come and play ball.

My friends fanned out in the field with Skip at their heels, and I started hitting fly balls to them, each in his own turn. With the first clean crack of bat against ball I began to relax, forgetting for the moment about witchcraft. Baseball is better than any demonology, and will probably last longer. There's nothing prettier than the long, casual arc of a baseball against an azure and driftless April sky. Henjie pounded his glove and made a snappy catch, losing his glasses in the process.

"Hummm-boy!" Bubba yelled.

They threw the ball around spiritedly to each other like infielders celebrating an out. Then Bubba tossed it back to me.

As I hit flies for them, the Yazoo River gently twisting and turning in the background, reflecting the distant sun in little priasmic sparkles, I lazily became aware of black kids materializing out of the distant pecan trees. Eight or nine boys and girls, little brothers and sisters tagging along, were suddenly standing there, waiting for us to invite them to play.

"Y'all come on out," Bubba called.

"Y'all want to get up a game?" I said, tossing up the ball and hitting one to Billy in centerfield. When he missed it, Skip retrieved it for him, dropping the ball from his mouth in front of Billy.

60

When I glanced around, the black kids were now standing about twenty paces closer. I'd hardly seen them move. When they saw me looking at them, the little kids fell to wrestling self-consciously and scuffling with each other, rolling on the ground and kicking up tiny clouds of dust. Eventually the biggest boy sidled up to me. I'd seen him before, but I didn't remember his name.

"I'm Ollie," he said.

"Hey, Ollie, I'm Willie. Ollie what?"

"Caruthers. Willie what?"

"Morris."

We appraised each other. He gestured toward his companions. "And he's Navy and he's Reginald and that's my little brother, Oscar."

Ollie and I continued to size each other up. We were about the same age. He wasn't quite as tall as I, but he was heavier. His skin wasn't black but the smooth rich color of milk chocolate. He was both foreign, and not. I felt a divide between us, but then again, I didn't. He wore a grey T-shirt and grimy khaki men's workpants that had been cut down in the legs. They were too big for him in the waist and were cinched tight with a piece of cord. The frayed bottoms flapped around his bare feet when he kicked at the dust. He saw me looking at his clothes and crossed his arms defensively. Behind him, his friends crossed their arms, too.

"Is that yo' *glove*?" he said disdainfully. My Rawlings baseball glove was lying on the ground beside me.

"Want to try it?" I said. "Go ahead."

He picked it up and slid his hand inside. When he pounded the pocket, his eyes lit up.

"That's all right," he said.

I thought, *I've got an old glove at home I don't use any more.*

"Y'all ready to play?" I said.

"Yeah," he said.

"Want to walk off the bases?"

61

"All right, we can use them sticks there for home plate and first, second, and third," he said.

Everybody got busy setting up a baseball diamond. The black kids had one more player than we did, excluding the little brothers and sisters, but that didn't matter. We agreed that their extra player would catch for both sides. They could bat first and use our gloves when we were at bat.

I started pitching, not throwing hard, giving them a chance to get into the rhythm. It felt good standing there in the warm stirring breeze from the river. The disrupting scene in the school assembly seemed far away. At first they swung wildly at every pitch, reaching for outside balls, and low ones, and striking out. But it didn't take the one named Ollie long to start hitting. He was a good natural athlete, a fast baserunner and quick fielder. I wished we had him on our team at school. After two innings, the score was 3-0 in our favor. They didn't seem to notice the score, or if they did, they didn't let on.

The next time Ollie came to bat, I decided to try out the curveball Daddy had taught me. I wrapped two fingers along the laces, the way I'd been instructed, snapped my wrist, and let fly. It broke sharply just before it crossed home plate. Ollie saw the ball coming at him and stepped away before it broke. His brother Oscar, who was catching for both teams, missed the catch and had to scramble after the ball.

"That was a *curve*," Ollie said.

"Never seen one before?" I called.

"Naw, throw me another one."

I saw him set himself to stand in against the curve. This time I threw a better breaking ball, a long, slow curve that tingled my wrist and sent little electric pulsations up my funny bone. "Don't throw many of those at your age," Daddy always said. "You'll throw out your arm." Ollie stepped into it and hit a strong line drive far over Bubba's head at second base. By the time Henjie ran it down in the weeds, Ollie had nearly rounded third base, his bare feet slapping the ground like thudding drumbeats. I covered home, pounding my glove and yelling for Henjie to throw it to me. All the little brothers and sisters were jumping up and down. Henjie's throw was a perfect one-hopper that I snagged near what would've been the baseline just as Ollie started to slide headfirst. We both dived toward the stick at the same time. I was sure I touched his leg with the ball before his hand found the stick. We sat up together in an angry cloud of dust.

"*Safe!*" Ollie cried, and looked at me with dusty eyebrows raised.

"Yeah, safe," I said. "Good hit."

"Naw, you tagged him out!" Bubba shouted. The black children grew quiet, watching and waiting.

"Tie goes to the runner," I said. "He's safe."

We played for a while longer, maybe an hour, maybe two. Nobody had a watch and time didn't matter, anyway. Then one of Ollie's friends had to take his little brothers home, and the game swiftly broke up. Ollie and I sat on the ground, chewing blades of grass and feeling friendly and relaxed.

"You're a good ball player," I said.

"I can hit your curve ball," he replied.

"Wait till I work on it," I said. "You ain't seen nothin' yet."

"I can still hit it."

"I got another ball glove at home," I said.

For a moment he didn't reply. "I can show you sump'm," he finally said.

"What?"

"You know all that devil bizness peoples be talkin' about?"

"Yeah!" I sat up straight. "What about it?"

"I know where they had one of them devil parties."

"You do! Where?"

"Come on. I'll show you."

"Where you going, Willie?" Bubba called.

"He's gonna show me something. Want to come?"

"Naw," Bubba said, "I'm hungry. I'm going home."

"Me, too," Henjie said.

"Me, three," Billy said.

"Okay, take my bat and glove for me, will you?" I asked Henjie. "I'll pick 'em up, later. Come on, Skip."

Ollie started walking off without saying anything. I hastened to follow him. He broke into a trot, as if he couldn't wait to show me something. We ran along a trail that led into the woods between cotton fields that started at the edge of this flat Delta land and would stretch like a pancake nearly to Memphis. Rows of new green cotton plants were growing out of the rich black earth all around us, as far as the eye could see, and gossamer clouds pressed tightly at the horizon. Ollie assumed a steady pace. I matched him stride for stride, with Skip not far behind. It felt fine to be trotting along beside him, going to a secret place. I saw smoke hanging in the air above the treeline at the farthest edge of the field.

"What's that?" I said.

"City dump," he replied.

I realized then that the black people had made a trail straight to the Yazoo garbage dump. I'd seen black men and women picking over the trash, before, when my daddy and I went to put some bags of garbage there. As we came through the trees I saw the endless piles of rotting garbage, heaps of old rubber tires and tin cans, slow fires burning and smoldering here and there like a war picture in the newsreels.

He led me past the dump into the woods near the river. The river itself was utterly deserted here, no boats nor fishermen, only the steady lonesome whine of it as behind the Clark Mansion and the dark brown impenetrable water, and the occasional gyrating limb or pieces of careless uninhibited flotsam and debris, and the gray-trunked cypresses with the water lapping about their knees. Always to me the river cypresses seemed bent down like wise men trying to tell me something, but on this day they were stark and threatening. Now we had no trail to follow and wound among tall trees, pecans and oaks and gums, going slower. A snake suddenly slithered out from the weeds, and we made a quick detour. Ollie didn't seem to mind going barefoot and I wondered if he owned a pair of shoes. His head, with its close-cropped, curly hair, bobbed up and down as he bent to avoid low-hanging branches and jumped like a gazelle over little precipitous ravines. After following the river bank for about twenty minutes we scrambled up a sharp, thorny ridge. On the other side of it we pushed through a canebrake and suddenly came into a hidden clearing.

"This is it," he said.

I looked around. At first there wasn't much to see except for empty beer cans and whiskey bottles and some burnt logs where a fire had been built in the middle of the clearing. Then he started poking around in the wild grass and weeds and showed me the bloody feathers, the blood now dried black and hard and covered with evil-smelling dust. We found a chicken's head with the comb still on it. Bones of larger animals had been strewn into the bushes. I mean real bones, of legs and necks and horrid fibulas, some with thin strands of flesh still attached to them. Were any of these bones *human*? Whoever had been here meant business. I came across a bloody piece of hairy skin that might've been part of a cat, or a possum, I couldn't tell. Skip sniffed at these, then whined and shrank away. All around this hideous site the grass and weeds were pressed low, as if having been trampled by many feet.

"They drinks the blood," he said, and a chill ran through me.

65

Was this it? I wondered. *Was this what we were getting ourselves into?*

"Ain't much to see now," he said, "but last week there was blood and feathers all over. They made a big mess, I tell you what."

"Who?"

"I don't know," he said. "Crazy peoples."

"Are you sure?"

"Sure I'm sure."

We kicked around in the grass and turned over the blackened logs. I began to imagine chants and shrieks in the night, unholy moans and incantations, suffering tremors and cries. I shivered again. What had we gotten into?

I picked up the chicken's head, brushing away some ugly bloated flies that had settled on it, holding it in careful horror between my thumb and index finger. As if by some weird osmosis, just touching it made my imaginings seem real. I succumbed to them. I thought I heard the chicken squawking, its wings beating the ground as unknown hands held it by its fluttering claws. An ax was raised, then swiftly flashed down, ending the poor bird's cries. The fire blazed up, reflecting wildly on faces painted red. A flute played a woeful melody, and masked figures appeared through the groundsmoke as though stepping out of the dark endless mouth of Hell. Someone held an executioner's sword menacingly over another sacrificial victim tied to a stake—only *this* was no chicken, or goat, or dog. It was a person. My mind's eye strained to identify the victim, who slowly turned toward me. Was she a girl? And from *town*?

"See where they drove a truck in here?" Ollie pointed to tracks among the trees.

"*What?*" I said, disoriented, still trapped in my blighted reverie.

"Them tracks there," he repeated. "See?"

"Oh, yeah." I was relieved to be back in the real world,

66

back with Ollie under green pines and blue sky, and the ripplings of the river, and Old Skip lying innocently in the grass, and the echo of a sawmill whistle far away. I took a closer look at the tracks he'd found. "It looks like they used it more than once," I said.

"Yeah, and they burnt more than one fire, too," he said.

"How do you know?"

"Look at the ash in the ground. It turned the dirt grey, see? The rain must've soaked it in."

"It hasn't rained in two weeks, except for a drizzle," I said. "How many times do you reckon they came here?"

"I don't know. But see where the ground's dented in—*right there*? They stacked logs right there. Can't you tell?"

"What did they need a lot of logs for?"

"I guess they wanted to keep the fire burnin' hot," he said.

"What's this?" I said, stooping to retrieve what looked like a black ball of wax.

"One of them black candles," he said.

I held the candle stub in my hand and examined it. The devil worshippers were said to burn black candles in celebrating the Black Sabbath. The silence of the big flat woods grew dense around me. From the farthest distance came the hoot of an owl, and then a solitary mourning dove. There was evil here. It hovered in the atmosphere. I could feel it.

My companion could too. The shadows were lengthening now, and a spooky haze was rising up from the river. "Let's go," he said.

Without another word he started back the way we'd come. I glanced around, half-expecting to see a devil's head ascend from the bushes, and then ran to catch up with him. Skip didn't want to stay either.

We headed to town at a faster clip than before. I was gasping for air by the time we reached the first cotton field, but neither of us wanted to stop until then. We slowed to a walk now, catching our breath. When we reached the city dump I saw the green hood of a car ease around one of the piles of smoking garbage. It was the sheriff's.

One of the deputies was behind the wheel. He stopped and called to us.

"What you boys doin' out here?"

"Nothing, sir. Just playing," I said, trying to look casual.

"Ain't you Ray Morris' boy?" he asked.

"Yessir."

"Who's that boy with you?"

"That's Ollie Caruthers."

"Well, go on back to town, now. This ain't no place for you boys to be hangin' around."

"Yessir," I said.

He drove away and left Ollie and me standing there listening to the owls and doves and whippoorwills. The smoke whirled all around us, and the sun descended across the Yazoo River, and a silvery little moon appeared from behind a thick pillowy cloudbank. I wasn't about to tell the deputy about the place we'd found in the clearing, the awful things we'd seen. It had been Ollie's secret–and mine–and I didn't want to share it, not even with Bubba, Henjie and Billy, my blood-brothers who'd signed X's on the Life-saver wrapper with me. Ollie looked at me.

"That was some curve ball," he said. "Didn't want to say it, before."

"You hit it out of the park," I said.

"Let's do it again, sometime."

"Okay."

"Be careful of all this scary stuff."

"You too."

"Well, so long, Willie."

"So long, Ollie."

We went our separate ways, I to the main road that led into town, Ollie to his trail in the woods that the black people had made.

68

Eight

THAT NIGHT I WAS sitting in the kitchen, reading Walter Stewart's sports column in the *Memphis Commercial Appeal* while Mama fixed supper and Daddy listened to Jack Benny on the radio. Old Skip, all tired out, was lying on the floor with his four paws extended upward. Mama was talking, talking, talking—about how people were keeping their children home from school tomorrow because of the fearsome rumors.

"Children aren't safe, anymore," she said, angrily stirring flour in a frying pan, making gravy. "Willie, I don't know if it's wise for you to go to school tomorrow. Did you hear me, Ray? Are you listening to me, Ray? —Oh, your daddy's doesn't listen to me."

I glanced up at Daddy over my newspaper. He winked at me and kept his ear toward the radio.

The phone rang. I went in the hall to answer it. It was Rivers.

"I picked out my dress for the Prom," she said. "I just thought you'd like to know."

"Oh, sure, that's great, Rivers." With everything going on, I'd forgotten all about the Prom.

"I don't care about a corsage," she said.

"What?"

"You know, a corsage. Some of the boys think they have to give them to their dates."

"Oh, yeah." *Dates.* Now it was sinking in on me, what I'd done. It would be like a real "date," and Mama would have to drive us. Everyone would see us getting out of the car, like little kids dressed up to play adults, and my mother behind the wheel.

"My daddy heard that the K.K.K.'s going to ride." Rivers changed the subject.

"Who?"

"The Ku Klux Klan, silly! They put out the word they're going to put an end to the devil worshippers and make the world safe for Christianity."

"How did your daddy find out about that?"

"It's all over town. Everybody's talking about what's going on. Are you going to school tomorrow?"

"Sure. Aren't you?"

"Yes. Will you walk me?"

"Okay, I guess." Were we going steady, I wondered? This was starting to confuse me. Rivers had always seemed so wonderfully cool, so, well, unattainable. Was she changing?

"You don't have to walk me, if you don't want to." A fine edge crept into Rivers' voice.

"That's okay. I want to!"

"Well, if you want to."

"Sure. It's fine."

"I'll see you tomorrow, then, Willie."

"Okay, Rivers."

"Sleep tight."

"Uh, uh, okay."

"Bye."

"Bye."

It made me feel kind of good to think about Rivers telling me to sleep tight, especially after the things I'd seen that day in the secret clearing which I was keeping all to myself. She'd never done that before. Come to think of it, the only reason she'd called me in the past was to ask about a homework assignment, or class project. It must be the Prom, I thought. She was acting strange.

"Mama?" I said when I went back to the kitchen. "How much does a corsage cost?"

A siren that wakes you out of a sound sleep in a small drowsing town in the deepest American hinterland in the dark rousing springtime cuts to the deepest quick. It's not a happy sound, not a spotted Dalmatian riding in a red firetruck kind of sound. Skip and I sat up in bed and looked at each other.

"What's *that*?" I said. "Come on Skip, something's happening."

A firetruck was coming. I heard its engine grinding underneath the wailing pulse of the alarm. I jumped out of bed and eased out the door of my room into the hall. The door to my parents' room was closed. Barefoot and wearing only the bottom half of my pajamas, I went out on the front porch and sat on the steps with my arm around Skip. He panted quietly, taking in this latest development with his usual calm interest. I was glad of his company.

The firetruck roared past our house on Grand Avenue, its silver wheels flashing mercurially in the light reflected from the corner streetlamp. After a moment we heard another siren. A smaller firetruck came by, followed by a police car with its red light flashing but without a siren. It didn't need to sound an alarm. There weren't any other cars on the road at that time of night, anyhow, and two sirens were a gracious plenty. I heard the sirens turn up the hill

71

past the cemetery. They were headed for the top of the ridge, where Miss Eddie Mack lived.

I tiptoed back inside the house—not to keep from waking my parents, because I knew they'd heard the noise, but to prevent them from knowing I was up at that hour, being three months shy of thirteen—and went to my room to get dressed. Skip walked so smoothly and quietly beside me it was like I had two big legs and four little ones. I pulled on my Yazoo Indians sweatshirt and a pair of jeans, stuck my feet in my hightop black tennis shoes and opened my door to listen. If Mama caught me, she'd make me go back to bed. Skip and I listened intently. I thought I heard Mama say something to Daddy and then his deep voice murmured sleepily, something like, "None of our business," and I imagined him turning over in bed.

I walked tactfully down the hall without a sound—heel and toe, Indian fashion—and went out the kitchen door, shutting it carefully behind me. Skip followed me to the garage to get my bike. Then we were off into the night, feeling cool and quick and sensing danger.

I peddled up the middle of the street like I owned it. At a time like this, in fact, Yazoo *did* belong to me, in a crazy kind of way. Nobody else was there to claim it and I was peddling for glory in the middle of the night. I was the Emperor of Yazoo and Skip was my first Viceroy.

Then we reached the cemetery.

There's nothing like being in a dark cemetery after midnight to make you appreciate being warm and comfortable in your own bed. The deep lush trees were like witches' caps, and the insects sang in gloomy cadence all about us, and the wrought-iron fences around the old family plots creaked in the ageless wind. I turned uphill, rocking back and forth on my handlebars and standing up on the peddles to put my weight into it. The rows of silent tombs seemed to be moving as I passed them, and the Witch's grave shimmered in the dim solemn moonlight. Skip ran

72

alongside me. I could see his mouth open, his teeth gleaming in the dark. He seemed to be saying, It ain't nothing but a lot of old graves, Willie, but let's keep moving anyhow.

There was a glare at the top of the hill, a garish pink glow that hovered menacingly above the trees. I realized, as I peddled, that I was looking at boiling smoke reflecting a fire beneath it. The solid dark shapes of the firetrucks hid Miss Eddie Mack's low sprawling house from view. Off to my right, the big tall trees in the wooded slopes across the ravine appeared to look down in grim disapproval. As the road grew steeper, I weaved back and forth to pick up momentum and get me to the top. Now I was close enough to hear men's voices yelling sharply. I saw their forms outlined in the red flashing light of the police car.

At the summit of the hill a flaming cross leaped out of the night. It stood like a burning tree, a giant warning hand ablaze in Miss Eddie Mack's front yard. There was something horrendous about using this gentle symbol of good will, this universal sign of Christ, as an instrument of terror. I leaned my bike against the fence and went around the hedge. Miss Eddie Mack was standing to one side, looking pale and frightened. But she was also mad as could be. Flames crackled and dense choking smoke swirled around me, and I lost sight of her face.

"Look out!" the fire chief shouted. "We're turnin' on the spray."

One of the firemen approached the burning cross and aimed a hose at it. The hose was attached to the portable water tank on the smaller firetruck. Up here on the ridge there was no fire hydrant for them to hook up a waterline to. I heard someone race the truck motor to wind up its pump. Then the spray came on and for a minute there was only the sizzling sound of water hitting fire.

The towering cross seemed to resist being extinquished. It blazed fiercely, then sputtered, then faltered, its flaming

73

arms reduced to humble little tongues of fire that were soon swallowed up by the greater darkness.

In the ensuing silence I heard Miss Eddie Mack's parrot squawking inside the house.

"The roof's caught!" the chief yelled. "Vern, put some spray on it. See where it is?"

The fireman turned the hose on some burning shingles. When he was finished, the parrot complained more loudly than ever. It must've thought the world was coming to an end.

"You act like it was my fault!" Miss Eddie Mack was saying to the sheriff. I moved closer to where she was standing under the bottle-tree.

"Now, now," he was saying.

"*You* catch the ones that did it!" she went on. "Catch them if you can."

"Well, the main thing is, nobody was hurt," the sheriff said. He glanced around awkwardly, as if looking for some excuse to elude her mounting anger. He seemed relieved to see me. "Who's *that*?" He came over to me.

"It's just me, Willie Morris, Sheriff," I said.

"What're you doing here?" he said. "Do your folks know you're here?"

"I heard the sirens," I said quickly. "I came to see what was going on. –Hey, Miss Eddie Mack."

"That's my *friend*," she said defensively. "He came to see about me. Leave him alone."

"I'm not doin' anything to him," the sheriff said. "Good grief, lady!" And he went to confer with the firemen, who were roaming about with flashlights in their hands making sure the fire was completely out. The cross was smoking and dripping like some bony dinosaur that men had killed, something that until recently had been very much alive.

"Can I do anything to help?" I asked.

"You can tell those people to get off my property!" Miss

74

Eddie Mack fumed. In the bizarre combination of red and white light, steam seemed to rise from her greying hair as if she, too, were smoking.

"Oh, they're just trying to help," I said, hoping that none of the officers had heard her. If they had, they weren't showing it.

"They think this is somehow my fault," she continued angrily. "Well, I don't need that kind of help."

"I think we've put the fire out now," the firechief said, sidling up warily toward the porch. He spoke to Miss Eddie Mack without looking at her, as though she might at any second bite him. "We'll come back in the morning and take the cross down for you."

"If you think someone did this to me to teach *me* a lesson, think again!" she said.

"I don't think nothin', ma'am," the firechief said defensively. "Nobody said nothin' against you."

"The sheriff was asking a lot of questions," she kept up her attack. "But they were the wrong questions. Don't ask why someone did this to *me*. Because that's what they want you to do. This was a diversion."

"Yes, ma'am—whatever you say, ma'am." The firechief was eager to get out of there. "Come on, boys, let's go," he called to his men.

"Look sharp you don't trample my plants!" Miss Eddie Mack yelled. "They're ruined as it is."

A truck motor raced as the firemen backed up and drove the larger truck down the hill. The sheriff stood waiting for the other firemen to roll up their hose. He didn't seem to want to have to speak with the lady of this house again.

"Look where they stamped on my herb garden," Miss Eddie Mack was complaining under her breath. "They don't care. It's all *weeds* to them. All of this! Just weeds."

I couldn't see anything in the dark. She must've had a kind of antenna that felt for her hurt plants. I remembered how she'd pointed them out to me earlier and how she

75

knew them each by name. The cross was dripping, and I could see that gasoline-soaked cloth had been wrapped around it. Someone had stuck it upright before lighting it, and whoever that someone was had unusual strength.

"It was *not* the Ku Klux Klan," Miss Eddie Mack said.

"Who?" I said.

"Whoever did that." She, too, was looking up at the lingering skeleton of a cross.

"Who was it, then?" I said, glancing over my shoulder as the other firetruck slowly drove away, followed by the sheriff's car. Without the pulsating light and siren, both vehicles seemed dull, merely functional and banal. It occurred to me that this was exactly what the police and firemen's roles were: they were doing their job. If it seemed exciting to me, that was because I didn't see it as protecting property, of fulfilling a duty to the frightened town. The glare of their headlights faded as the vehicles descended the hill and beyond the cemetery out of sight, leaving Miss Eddie Mack and me alone amid the screech of cicadas and the sullen *drip, drip, drip* from the cross.

"They want to throw the law off the trail," she said at last.

"Who does?"

She took a deep breath and turned to me briskly. "Well, it's over, for the time being. You better go on home, boy. But I thank you for coming. You have a good heart."

"Who was it?" I persisted. "Who wanted to throw them off the trail?"

"*Them*," she said.

And without another word she disappeared into her house. A moment later I saw a light come on in one of the rooms. I looked up at the cross gauntly outlined against the sibilant midnight sky. Still smoking, it seemed to be panting sullenly, waiting for those who had created it to return and ignite it, bring it roaring back to life. *If it wasn't the Ku Klux Klan*, I thought, *who did it?*

76

I looked around for Skip and felt him brush against my leg. In all the excitement I'd forgotten about him, but of course, he'd not forgotten me.

"Come on, Old Skip," I said. "Let's go home."

Nine

AFTER THE CROSS-BURNING, pandemonium broke loose in Yazoo. Across the sweep of time, these tormented days were among the worst in its long and flamboyant history. Its people would remember them as long as people remember.

School attendance was down by 35% the very next day. Parents were afraid their children would be snatched off the street by anonymous devil worshippers roaming—I reckon—in broad daylight. A *bomb* threat was phoned in to the principal's office, and for an hour and a half the students milled around in the schoolyard waiting for the police to search the building. No one knew who was responsible, but I figured some kid, bored at staying home with nothing to do, must've done it.

Why would the real devil worshippers waste their time with bomb threats? That wasn't their style.

The students were titillated by all the ruckus. The younger boys were hiding behind trees, then jumping out

78

and trying to scare somebody, becoming playground devils. Girls screamed and laughed. It was contagious. I thought, *They're enjoying this.*

The police were not amused, however. There must have been a great deal of pressure on them to "save the town," because that evening they increased their patrols and surrounded a suspicious van parked on Lover's Lane. It turned out to be Mr. Silas Holly, who owned the Piggly Wiggly Store, necking with his checkout girl.

Later, the sheriff received a tip that witches were holding a ritual with a "vicious pack of dogs." He and his men sneaked up to the bosky place with pistols drawn and, sure enough, there were men, women and children leading dogs around on leashes, chanting in unison something like *"Zitt, oodaw, ow-zay!"* While the deputies slipped behind a fence and got into position, Sheriff Biggers turned on his bullhorn and told the devil worshippers to stay where they were—they were under arrest.

The dog-handlers remained right where they were, all right. When the deputies converged on them, Mrs. Elvira Nix, President of the Yazoo Canine Club, explained that they were holding a dog obedience class. Before the sheriff's men had so rudely interrupted them, they'd been teaching the command: "Sit, good dog. Now, stay!"

The mayor's office announced that a town meeting would be held Thursday night to clear the air. I thought this was a sensible idea. People were spreading rumors about Miss Eddie Mack and this worried me.

Thursday afternoon, on the way home from school, Rivers was waiting for me with Skip, who'd come to meet me at his usual sidewalk crack. The three of us strolled along together. I liked the sound of our shoes scuffing the pavement and the clicking of Skip's paws, which reminded me that his nails needed trimming.

"We're decorating the Country Club tonight," Rivers said. "Want to come?"

"The town meeting's tonight," I said.

"Why do you want to go to an old town meeting?" Rivers was almost pouting. I couldn't believe it. She seemed changed, somehow, charged with energy, with determination and soulful verve. Her cheekbones were more pronounced, her eyes greener, her smooth skin flushed. What was happening to Rivers?

"I ought to be there," I said stubbornly.

"*Why?*"

"Well, why do you have to decorate the Country Club?"

An icy space of arctic air suddenly opened up between us. Skip trotted on ahead to get out of our way. He was always so reasonable, Skip was.

"I don't *have* to," she said calmly. "I *want* to."

"The Prom's mainly for juniors and seniors," I went on, unable to stop myself. "They don't want seventh graders hanging around."

Rivers spun about to face me. She was so beautiful when she got mad. Her eyes grew dark, with little gold flecks in them.

"Is that so?" she said. "Well, for your information, Bobby Shoemaker asked me for a date last week."

A vacant, hollow feeling welled up in me. Bobby Shoemaker was a star halfback and president of the "Y" Club. Ole Miss had already offered him a football scholarship. I shuffled along, pretending that I didn't care. Rivers matched me step for step.

"Willie, you need to get your priorities straight."

"*Priorities!*" I immediately scratched my neck, which always started itching when life got complicated.

"Sure, priorities, you know."

"I never thought about priorities. I don't think I have any."

"Everybody ought to have priorities, Mama says. You better get some."

I glanced petulantly at Rivers. "What did you tell Bobby Shoemaker?"

"Him?" Rivers smiled to herself. "I told him I already had a date."

"*With who!*"

"With you, silly." She punched me in the arm, not hard. I was grinning like a clown. Then Rivers said, "Did you hear about the cross being burned at the Witch's house?"

"She's no witch!" I exclaimed.

Rivers glanced at me narrowly. "Well, that's what people say."

"I don't care what people say. I'm *tired* of hearing about what everybody says. Miss Eddie Mack's not a witch."

"What makes you so sure?"

"She told me."

Rivers stopped in the middle of the sidewalk and stared at me. Skip sniffed diplomatically around a rose bush in a lady's yard.

"You went to her *house*?" Rivers said.

"I was there when the cross was burned," I said.

"Willie!"

"I mean, I got there just after the fire truck did. I heard the sirens and followed them up there."

"It was midnight," she said.

"So what?"

She regarded me uneasily. "I wish you'd go decorate the Country Club with me and not go to that town meeting."

"I'm sorry, Rivers. I can't."

"Willie, you're not responsible for what people say about Miss Eddie Mack. I wish you'd forget about that."

"I can't," I said, and looked around for something to change the subject. "Look at Old Skip! He's not worried."

And we watched Skip follow a scent along the base of a hedge, his tail wagging to beat the band.

About six that evening, the citizens began to gather at the Courthouse. Rooks and swallows circled the clock

81

tower, seeking a temporary roost. Usually at about this time people had just finished eating supper and were sitting on their front porches or listening to Fibber McGee and Molly on the radio or just talking and watching the cars go by. Instead, here the citizens of Yazoo were, entering the courthouse on a ponderous mission. The men, who probably felt more comfortable behind their cash registers or desks, seemed uncharacteristically out of place. The women, however, girded their indignation about them and marched into the building as if *they* knew how to confront a crisis, even if they'd never faced one quite like this before.

I came with my parents but immediately separated from them as we approached the Courthouse. Bubba, Billy and Henjie were waiting for me, looking pretty nervous.

"We ought not to be here," Bubba said as soon as I came up to them. His face looked like it was screwed on wrong. He kept twisting his head as though to set it right. "We did some bad things."

"In a good cause," I said.

"People will get suspicious," Henjie said..

"Maybe we could sit in different seats," Billy suggested.

"I just got here," I said. "Come on."

We went inside and climbed the stairs to the courtroom. The old hallways smelled of dust and chewing tobacco and vintage spittoons and stale cigarettes, the subtle accumulated layers of age and distress. Inside the packed courtroom, women were fanning themselves with cardboard fans or magazines or their hands. Though it was unseasonably cool outside, the brick Victorian building retained the heat of the day, now augmented by two hundred people crowded hip to thigh into the rows of bench-type seats. I sniffed ladies' drugstore perfume, men's aftershave, snuff, juicy fruit gum and a faint but unmistakable aura of bourbon. The Devil might be whirling around the Courthouse steeple, right now, and somewhere

82

out in the county nameless and marginal and hateful men might be wrapping cloth on wooden crosses and unscrewing the caps of gasoline cans, but here in the bosom of Yazoo at least the world *smelled* normal.

My friends and I sat on the back row next to some old men who reminded me of the Amen corner at church where the elder deacons dozed off regularly. These old fellows seemed to be waiting patiently for the meeting to get started so they could go to sleep.

The majority of the audience, however, were staring curiously at the man the mayor escorted to the dais. He was a stocky, athletic-looking man, a little younger than my daddy– maybe thirty-five or so–with a natural air of suppressed authority and a little brown birthmark on his left earlobe. The audience looked him over with mixed expressions of optimism and disdain.

"Are you looking for your mom and dad?" Bubba whispered. "They're sittin' over there."

"Naw, I was looking for Miss Eddie Mack," I said. "I don't think she's here."

Then the mayor stood to open the meeting.

"I'd like to thank y'all for coming out tonight," he began. "This is an unusual situation, and it calls for cooperation and understanding. With us tonight is Lieutenant Rodney McDowell of the Mississippi Bureau of Investigation. Lieutenant McDowell has come over here from Jackson to help put things into perspective. So without further ado, I'll turn the program over to him. Lieutenant?"

The mayor stepped back and the state investigator advanced to the podium. There was scattered applause, not all that enthusiastic. The lieutenant looked around briskly at the waiting crowd.

"Thank you, Mr. Mayor," he said. "It's nice to be back in Yazoo..."

Women paused in fanning themselves and glanced at

83

each other as if to say, *Nice? Child sacrifice is a nice occasion to be back?*

"I see some familiar faces out there," the visitor went on. "As some of you may recall, I was assigned to this area when I first started working for the Bureau. Ordinarily, folks in my line of business avoid publicity like the plague, but tonight I'd like to go on record about the problem that's been bothering this community lately."

The lieutenant began to discuss witchcraft so openly and casually he might've been a game warden talking about wildlife management, or a dermatologist about high school pimples. I could see how shocked some of the ladies were. They'd no doubt expected the officials to echo their own feverish outrage. Instead, here was this investigator from the state capital talking about witches and demonology as though they were mere bugs under a microscope.

"While demonology isn't commonly practiced in our state," he said, "it's not unusual in certain New England states and also in California. Everything happens in California."

"Is it legal?" a man called out.

"Yessir, it is," the lieutenant said soberly, "as long as the cult abides by the letter of the law and doesn't disturb the peace."

"Is makin' bloody signs and hangin' dead crows from a flagpole disturbin' the peace'?" someone else shouted.

A hubbub of agreement arose en masse. My friends and I glanced at each other. We were sitting on the edge of our seats. Around the chamber women continued to fan themselves with renewed impatience.

"Well, technically that's a misdemeanor," Lt. McDowell said, calm as could be, "and the perpetrators are definitely in violation of city ordinances."

"They oughta be thrown in jail!" a lady cried.

I looked to see who had spoken and was amazed that it was Mrs. Gladys Brooks, a piano teacher who was my

84

mother's main rival for music students in Yazoo. Usually she was as serene as a meadowlark. Now her face was high crimson, and perplexed.

"Well, ma'am, I agree they should be apprehended and prosecuted to the full extent of the law. As to practicing witchcraft, however, I must tell you that those individuals are protected by the First Amendment to the United States Constitution just like everybody else."

An irate muttering filled the courtroom, rising and falling like a crescendo of muffled thunder, and the lieutenant raised his hand.

"Folks, let me assure you," he said, "that every effort is being made to put an end to the harassment your community's been enduring. I'm working closely with Sheriff Biggers, and I guarantee you he's on top of the situation. He has some further information, and I'd like to turn the meeting over to him now."

The sheriff reluctantly approached the podium.

"We been collectin' evidence on witchcraft activity in this county for some time now," he said in a low, brusque voice.

There was a collective intake of breath, and all the fans paused simultaneously.

"Some kinda cult has apparently been operatin' around here for over a year," Biggers went on.

Suddenly the courtroom exploded. People were on their feet shouting in disbelief. The atmosphere was belligerent with unbridled hostility. I sat still, thinking of the secret clearing Ollie had shown me, the burnt logs, the black candle stub, the dismembered beasts. Who was out there and why did they do what they did? *That* was what people were really afraid of, I thought, the unknown.

"If you know about this, why didn't you put a stop to it?" Mrs.Brooks cried accusingly.

"Now, now, Mrs. Brooks," the Sheriff said.

"Don't you *now-now* me!" she retorted, and the audience laughed in hot and democratic relief.

"The truth is," the Sheriff explained, "I can't go around arrestin' every Tom, Dick and Harry that dances around a campfire and hollers at the moon. If I did, I'd have to arrest half the coonhunters and trotline fishermen in Yazoo County. If a man ain't breakin' the law, I can't arrest him. That's all there is to it."

"Why wasn't this information brought out before now?" a man loudly demanded.

"Far as I was concerned," the sheriff said, hitching up his belt and scratching his ear, "it wasn't nobody's business if some folks wanted to dress up in strange clothes and beat on drums and carry on, not if they wasn't hurtin' nobody."

"Even if they were *crazy!*" a woman cried.

"I'm no doctor," the sheriff shrugged, "and that's not for me to say. I ain't elected to examine people's *brains*. All I know is, if they ain't strictly breakin' the law, I have to leave 'em to their business, whether I agree with 'em or not."

"*Tell us who they are!*" a man demanded. There was a bloodthirsty tone in his voice that sent a chill up and down the room.

"I'm not sure that'd be in *anybody's* best interests," the sheriff replied.

"You don't know, or you ain't tellin'?" the same man persisted.

Vociferous shouts bounced off the ceiling. Women dropped their fans as if ready to give in to the heat and let it blaze. Everyone was standing, except for the old men on the back row next to us. They were, however, wide awake. They craned to try to see around the people standing in front of them. One of them glanced hopefully at me to relate what was happening. I started to speak to him, then heard a woman shout:

"*Is it Edwina McBride?*"

86

I climbed on the bench to see who had spoken. Bubba yanked at me to pull me down. I made him turn loose and stood up on the bench again. I didn't care who saw me. Miss Eddie Mack wasn't present to defend herself. If she'd been here, she would've spoken out. She wasn't afraid of anybody. Well, maybe not anybody, I thought, remembering the burning cross.

Them, she had said.

"I don't know who it is!" the sheriff said. "And if I did, I wouldn't tell you."

Now there were other cries: *He's an elected official!* and *Has a responsibility to the voters who elected him!*

Sheriff Biggers swallowed his irritation and said, "Everything possible's bein' done to clear up this situation, folks. Everything's under control. Lieutenant, did you have anything else to say?" The sulky undercurrent of complaints continued as the investigator returned to the podium.

"I'd like to reiterate what Sheriff Biggers has said," he called out to be heard over the low petulant murmur. "There's no need for panic. Anyone who breaks the law will be arrested, you can be sure of that. Let me say, however, that a more serious problem in this county is the illegal production and distribution of alcohol. It's a criminal outrage, perpetrated by dangerous men. We don't know who they are. If anyone has any information about a group of individuals engaged in illegal manufacture and distillation of alchohol, the Bureau would appreciate his coming forward with such information."

The meeting began to break up. The mayor started to thank everyone for coming, but the perplexed citizens were already testily filing out the double doors at the rear of the courtroom.

While waiting to leave I overheard a woman telling her companion: *Let 'em have their moonshine but catch the devil worshippers.*

87

Another: *I can't believe the sheriff knew about them and didn't do anything about it.*

And a man: *Biggers ought to be voted out of office.*

I glanced toward the front of the courtroom and saw the mayor and sheriff shaking hands with the lieutenant. Nobody went up to speak to them or to thank them. All three of them glanced at the retreating flocks of Yazooans defensively. Surely this was more than they'd bargained for. I felt a little sorry for them. They were doing the best they could.

...a more serious problem in this county.

The lieutenant's admonition resounded in my mind. I had no idea why I remembered it so clearly. I left the courtroom and went to find my friends, who were waiting for me on the courthouse lawn under the statue of the Confederate soldier.

"Whew! I'm glad that's over," Henjie said.

"Yeah, now we can go home and listen to 'Yours Truly, Johnny Dollar,' " Billy said.

"Not yet," I said. "We've got some unfinished business."

"Oh, boy," Bubba moaned. "I was afraid you'd say that."

Ten

WE WENT TO BUBBA'S house because his folks were among
the most liberal parents in Yazoo, and they never seemed
to mind a cadre of boys underfoot after dark, even in this
spooked-up and unmanageable springtime. When we got
there Bubba's mother asked what we were up to, just for
the conversation, and Bubba told her we were making
plans for the Prom and that it wouldn't take long.

Bubba's parents had built a game room for him over
their garage, and we liked to hang out there. Billy and
Henjie immediately picked up cue sticks and started
shooting pool on the fullsized billiard table covered with
green felt just like the ones at Bailey's Pool Hall.

I found a pencil and a piece of paper in a cupboard drawer
and sat crosslegged on the leather sofa to make notes.

"What're you doin', Willie?" Bubba said.

"Making a list of suspects," I said.

"Suspects! Like the police do?" Bubba exclaimed, perch-
ing on the side of the pool table.

"Move, Bubba," Henjie said. "You're blockin' my shot."

"The witch goes at the top of that list," Billy said, chalking his cue stick with his eyes screwed up to judge a shot, like some pool shark from Memphis. He saw me glancing at him in irritation. "Oh, I know you and her are big buddies and all…"

"We're not buddies," I cut in. "But she's no witch, either."

"It was *your* idea to make a list," Billy persisted. "I vote we put her on it."

"Okay, okay," I said, writing *Miss Eddie Mack* on the piece of paper. "But just because she's first on the list doesn't make her the prime suspect. Now, anybody got any other ideas?" There was a moment of solemn reflection in which the only sound was the click of Billy's cuestick against the billiard ball, and a mockingbird singing from down the lane.

"There's Mr. Schwarz, the jeweler," Bubba said.

"What, just because he's German?" I said.

"What, just because he's German?" Billy mimicked.

"Yeah, put him down," Henjie said.

"Okay, okay," I said and wrote *Mr. Schwarz* on the paper. "But he didn't even like the Nazis."

"How do you know?" Henjie asked.

"Because he bought war bonds."

Then Billy thought of "Old Phil," the town drunk, who always loitered at the bus station with a bottle of cheap whiskey in his pocket. He stayed passed out half the time. The police generally left him alone because he smelled so bad he stunk up the jail whenever they arrested him for vagrancy, and because he talked in his sleep and moaned away in the nights.

"He's not sober enough to practice secret rites," I protested.

"What, just because *you* didn't think of him?" Billy said.

"Booze is probably a requirement for worshipping the Devil," Bubba said.

"Okay, okay," I said, and wrote *Phil* on my list.

Then Bubba reminded us of Royal Porter, a taxi driver who cruised about town slumped at his wheel looking forever unkempt and deranged. Even though he ran a taxi, Old Skip was a better driver than he was. Rumor had it that he was the delivery man for the local bootleggers. And Henjie pointed out that Mr. Bailey, who operated the pool hall, was no saint either. And Mr. Holmes Lane, the mortician, was pretty strange too.

"Wait a minute," I said, putting the paper and pencil aside. "What you're saying is that these people ought to be suspects because they're *different* from everybody else?"

"So was Jack the Ripper," Henjie said, sighting down his cue stick with a prideful smirk.

"If you're gonna make a list," Bubba put in, "you have to start somewhere, don't you?"

"Okay," I said, "then since we're puttin' down people of different natures than most, I have a prime suspect for you: *Spit McGee.*"

Now it was their turn to protest. Billy and Henjie lowered their cue sticks and argued with me. No, no, they said, not old Spit. Not good old Spit.

"What's fair is fair," I said. "Just because Spit's our friend doesn't mean we can look the other way. Remember, Spit's been absent from school for a month. He told us he's been working for his daddy—which can mean doing just about anything—and it was Spit that told us about the star in a circle."

I picked up the pencil and held it poised above the paper. They looked warily at each other.

"I can't see Spit dancing and singing hymns to the Devil," Bubba said.

I went ahead and added Spit's name to the list. The scratching of my pencil was the only sound in the room now. Then I held up the paper and read what I'd written:

Suspect	Occupation	Suspicious Behavior
1) *Miss Eddie Mack*	–widow, lives alone	–general principles
2) *Mr. Schwarz*	–jeweler	–he's German
3) *Phil*	–town drunk	–doesn't give a damn
4) *Royal*	–taxi driver	–looks suspicious
5) *Mr. Bailey*	–runs pool hall	–shady connections
6) *Mr. Lane*	–funeral home	–acts funny
7) *Spit McGee*	–playing hooky	–circled star sign

Billy put down his cuestick. "It's radio time–'Yours Truly, Johnny Dollar,' " he said.

"*Wait a minute*," I said.

"That show comes on Wednesdays," Henjie corrected Billy. "Tonight's 'Mr. District Attorney.' "

"Oh, yeah," Billy said.

"Come on, fellas," I said. "We haven't finished our list."

" 'Inner Sanctum' is on at ten," Billy said.

I jumped up and waved the paper at them. Bubba stood by the door and gave me a forbidding look, like I had leprosy, or tick fever.

"What about our list?" I repeated.

"Okay, I'd like to add another name," Bubba said mysteriously.

"Who?" I said, encouraged by his new interest.

"Willie Morris, white male, age twelve and about a half, weight approximately seventy-five, height five foot one..."

"...and a quarter," I interjected, enjoying what I thought was a joke.

"Occupation: baseball and pranks," Bubba continued, and he wasn't smiling one bit. "Suspicious behavior: nothin' much except he writes signs in blood and runs dead crows up school flagpoles."

"*Wait a minute*." I looked at Bubba, then at Henjie and Billy. They weren't smiling either. "I don't believe this," I said. "You don't think *I'm* a witch?"

"The word is *warlock*," Henjie said.

"If Spit McGee's a suspect just for telling us how to draw

a witch's star," Bubba was unrelenting, "why shouldn't *you* be?"

"What about you and Henjie and Billy!" I yelled, trying to keep my voice from squeaking in righteous disbelief at this sudden inquisition. "You want me to write *your* names, too?"

"*We* didn't think of none of those shananigans," Bubba said. "You did."

I looked at the others and saw from their noncommittal expressions that Bubba spoke for them too. It was a horrifying consensus.

"Hey, we're in this together," I said. "Remember the oath we took?"

"That oath was your idea," Henjie said.

"Fact is, all this witch stuff's your idea," Billy said.

"It was not," I said.

"Whose was it, then!" Bubba said.

Just then Bubba's mother came to say that Henjie's mother had phoned and wanted to know when he was coming home.

"I'm gone!" Henjie said. He put his cue stick in the rack and without so much as a farewell stormed out into the night.

Then Billy took off, too, and Bubba said goodbye, and soon I was walking up Grand Avenue by myself.

It was very dark and the stars were pale frescoes amid the drifting clouds. The air was heavy with the honeysuckle and wisteria, and a quivering quarter moon was rising over the windless treetops. I could see people inside their lighted houses, going from room to room or reading their newspapers. Somebody was practicing an offkey saxophone. Nobody saw me walking up the sidewalk. I could've been invisible.

Glancing up I saw a low, flat wisp of cloud float past the moon. I squinted and made the cloud take on different

93

shapes. Was it a witch on a broomstick? Was it a headless horseman? Was it a giant bat?

"*Hey, Willie.*"

I nearly jumped out of my skin. A shadowy figure emerged from the bushes by the sidewalk.

"Is that you, Spit?" I said. "What're you doing here?"

"I reckon I can come into town whenever I want to," he said, and spat some tobacco juice on the curb. "Want a chew?"

"No, thanks. Better not let the truant officer see you."

"Age limit for leavin' school is sixteen," he said, grinning. "Won't be too long 'fore I'm *legal*. Anyways, I been lookin' for you, Willie."

"What for?" I said.

"Y'all did such a good job on that ol' sign on the Clark Mansion, I thought you'd like to be in another stunt."

"What is it?" I couldn't help being curious.

"About that Prom y'all are havin'," he said. "I hear the whole town'll be there."

"Just about," I said.

At that moment a car drove by, and Spit led me into the bushes so nobody would see us talking. We crouched there and looked at each other.

"I got me an idea," he said.

Eleven

I SAT ON THE passenger's side of our car while my mother drove up Grand Avenue at a rapid pace. We were late, as usual. My starched collar made my neck itch, but when I tried to tug at my bowtie, Mama reached over without looking away from the road and slapped at my hand.

"Don't do that," she said, "you'll make your tie crooked."

I was wearing new grey slacks and a navy blue sports jacket, a black and yellow bowtie and saddle oxfords that Old Skip had watched me polish to a faretheewell. In my lap I held a wrist corsage made of gardenias. My daddy had given me two dollars to buy it at the floral shop next to the Catholic church. I could've selected carnations, but gardenias smelled like Rivers sometimes did, when she was not sweating. Tonight, Friday, April 7, 1946, was the night of the Yazoo High Senior Prom. We were on our way to Rivers' house to pick her up.

"Oh, your cowlick's sticking up again," Mama said, digging into her purse with one hand while steering with the other. The Desoto veered across into the opposite lane.

"Look out, Mama!" I yelled.

"Here, let me comb it for you," she said, producing a plastic comb from her purse and reaching for my hair.

"No, please don't!" I said.

"Be still," she said, and the Desoto continued to wobble from the curb to the center stripe like a ship in distress while she stroked the comb through my hair. I squeezed over next to the door, but Mama had long arms for a pretty woman and there was no escape.

"It doesn't matter!" I protested.

"Yes, it does," she said determinedly. "You want to look your best, don't you? That cowlick's standing up like the devil, boy. It's got a mind of its own. Never saw such a cowlick. Well, that's the best I can do. You do look handsome, even if your hair sticks up. Everybody's going to say Willie Morris is the handsomest boy at the dance."

"Oh, Mama!" I moaned.

"But I don't want you wandering around outside the Country Club," she went on. I noticed that the Desoto continued to drift to and fro within the limits of the right lane. "They're going to have extra chaperones, and the police are going to be on patrol, due to all the talk about the devil worshippers grabbing some poor girl–or boy!–but I want you to be careful and stay inside. You *and* Rivers. Do you hear me? Charles Applewhite will drive out to pick you up at eleven..."

"Twelve!" I broke in. "Twelve!"

"No, we agreed that..."

"The band plays till midnight," I said.

And something else was to happen at midnight.

"If he goes to get you at eleven-thirty, he can beat the traffic. Be reasonable, boy. This is your first Prom. There will be a lot more when you can stay out late. You're not even thirteen yet."

96

It was bad enough that Rivers and I had to be delivered to the Senior Prom by my mother, like a couple of little kids going to a birthday party, without being seen leaving *early*. Grownups never understood the significance of these situations. Would they ever? I was trying to establish myself among my elders. My girl–that is, the girl who would be my girl as soon as I could afford to *have* a girl–had already been asked out by Bobby Shoemaker, a *senior* classman and football player. If Rivers and I were seen waiting in front of the Country Club for Mr. Applewhite to pick us up at *eleven-thirty* I was dead at Yazoo Junior High.

"Here we are," Mama said, turning into the Applewhites' driveway. "I'll wait while you go to the door to get her. Now remember your manners." I started to get out of the car. "Wait," she added, reaching for her comb again. "Maybe I can get that old cowlick to stay down for a minute or two."

"It's all right!" I got out fast, eluding her relentless assault.

I went to the door, feeling the starched front of my shirt bending against my stomach like armor plating, and rang the doorbell. I sort of hid the corsage, in its clear plastic container, behind my back. Rivers' mother and father were waiting to inspect me. I braced myself for this new ordeal. Was any Prom worth this agony? Then the door opened, and Mr. Applewhite was grinning down at me–was that *sympathy* I saw in his eyes?–and asking me to come in. He offered me his hand, as if we hadn't met until just this minute, and I shook it ceremoniously, as I assumed the occasion demanded. That handshake set the tone. We were now officially strangers. Mrs. Applewhite, however, seemed much more at ease. She beamed at me and reached out–I guess all mothers have to do this, they can't help themselves–and picked some lint off my navy jacket. What would mothers do without lint? She told me I looked swell and that Rivers would be right down. We went into their living room, and Mr. Applewhite invited me to sit on their sofa. I felt a drop of sweat run down my back. I could think of nothing to say, not a single word in the whole of the English tongue, not one.

"Rivers says the party's over at twelve," Mr. Applewhite said.

Thank you, Sir. Thank you! Oh, Wise, oh, Benevolent! I thought to myself in a warm rush of gratitude.

"Yessir," I said. "Right at twelve. Well, maybe a few minutes after."

"Then that's when I'll be coming to get you," he added. "Just look for my car. I'll be lined up with all the others, probably out on Country Club Road. By that time the loop in front of the building will be jammed."

"Yes, sir, we'll be there," I said.

I heard a rustle of starched petticoats on the staircase. And then Rivers was standing at the door to the hall. Mr. Applewhite and I stood, together, and stared in mutual admiration.

There's something about a girl in a white dress, I've learned, no matter what her age. I stood rooted to the floor, devoid of speech, of movement, of conscious thought. All that remained was feeling. Just looking at her dressed up like that, so stunningly pretty that it hurt me, I felt the roof of my mouth all parched and dry.

"Hi, Willie!" she said brightly. Her voice sounded so normal. How could she be so calm? "Well, I'm ready," she added.

"Okay," I said. "Let's go." Then I remembered the corsage and abruptly held it out to her. "Here, Rivers."

"Oh, Willie, *thank* you! Look, Mama. A corsage!"

While I dawdled by the door, anxious to get outside, to let the cool night assuage my unfamiliar emotions, to put some distance between me and the place where I'd had this rude and funny awakening, Mrs. Applewhite and Rivers attached the corsage to her wrist, and Rivers looked in the hall mirror adjusting it. After a few moments she was ready to go. I was standing by the door, holding it open for her. Mr. Applewhite reminded me of where he'd be waiting to pick us up. And then we were *outside*, together, Rivers' skirt swishing against my trousers leg as we went down the walk to the driveway. I almost felt grown up, except that at the end of the walk, there was my mother's face, framed and waiting in the driver's window.

"Aren't they the handsomest couple in town!" Mama shouted to the Applewhites, who were peeking out the door at us. Anybody within a mile or two could've heard her. My face was burning as I escorted Rivers around to the other side of the car and opened the front door for her. There was hardly room for the three of us to sit abreast in the front seat, especially with Rivers' dress taking up so much room. But I would've let the most fiendish of devil worshippers burn me at the stake before I'd be driven to the Country Club sitting in the *back seat* with Rivers.

Mama talked the entire time it took to drive out to the club. The rumors were that the demonologists planned to make a ritual sacrifice that night, which happened to be Good Friday. This was already common knowledge. Many parents were frantic about their offsprings' safety. Rivers and I just sat there, listening to my mother lecture us about staying inside and not wandering around on the golf course and minding what the chaperones said. I secretly inhaled Rivers' perfume. Her own scent and that of the corsage joined the mingling cachet of Southern springtime. It made me dizzy to be sitting so close to her. What a combination: my mother's endless advice and Rivers' sweet, fresh fragrance. It was enough to warp a fellow for life. There was a long line of cars in front of the driveway leading up to the imposing oak bungalow. Mama stopped the car and disengaged the clutch, idling the motor. I seized the opportunity to save whatever face I had left.

99

"We'll just get out here and walk the rest of the way," I said, opening the door as quickly as I could.

"Rivers might get her dress dirty," Mama protested.

"It's all right, Mrs. Morris," Rivers said, sliding out behind me. "We can walk on the gravel shoulder. Thanks for bringing us. 'Bye now!"

And so we made our getaway, while Mama gunned the motor and tried to negotiate a U-turn in the face of the oncoming traffic. I heard her brakes squeal as a car stopped shortly to let her into the line of vehicles headed back into town. There wasn't room on the gravel shoulder for both of us to walk side by side, so I went a little ahead and Rivers followed. I felt I was leading Cinderella to the royal ball, and the gravel I crunched underfoot could have been *diamonds*.

Although I didn't have a watch, it must've been about a quarter until eight, when the music was scheduled to begin. Traditionally the senior class hired the most famous band in the Delta, the Redtops. They were Negro singers who combined their native blues with a swingband beat, but the Redtops transcended any race, color or creed. From the first note to the last, they were a world unto themselves.

I noticed that, though some cars we passed were driven by students with their dates, many of the drivers were parents. Even upperclassmen were being chauffered by their elders. This made me feel better, regardless of the reason, which of course was the Devil threat. Extra policemen directed traffic and parked their conveyances conspicuously near the manicured front lawn of the club. An officer stopped each car as it turned into the club driveway and shined his flashlight on the occupants. As we walked past a squad car, I heard the police radio squawk through the open window. Some officer was joking about being on "demon patrol."

Out in front of the building, Henjie and Bubba and Billy

were standing around pretending not to have seen me coming. I suppose they wondered if I was angry at them for deserting me. Well, I might've been, if not for the dark stunt Spit McGee and I'd planned the night before in the bushes. They looked as stiff and uncomfortable in their coats and ties as I. Bubba was the only person in sight wearing a white dinner jacket. Sometimes it didn't pay to have the richest parents in town. I waved at them to come over and speak to us, and then they saw Rivers. I had to smile at their undisguised expressions of regard.

Is that Rivers? Good golly, Miss Molly, she is one good-looking girl. Did we say girl? Look again.

Bubba finally spoke. "Willie," he said, drawing me to the side after greeting Rivers, "kids're pumped up about the devil worshippers. They're sayin' the witches have planned a main event for tonight."

"Yeah," Henjie put in excitedly, "and five hunnerd people are coming from Louisiana and Arkansas and Alabama to join in the sacrifice. Even as far away as Kentucky."

"Sacrifice?" I said, feigning a tepid interest. "What sacrifice?"

"Four young girls," Bubba whispered.

"Hey, you don't really believe that, do you?" I said, enjoying myself now that the tables were so irrevocably turned.

"Guys are packin' pistols tonight," Henjie said before Bubba could reply.

"Pistols!" Now I was surprised. "*Real* pistols?"

"Bobby Shoemaker's got a twenty-two automatic tucked under his cumberbund," Bubba said. "He showed it to some fellows a while ago in the lockerroom. It's not very big but it's *mean*."

I glanced out at the smoothly tossing golf course. I could see the first green shining with dew in the moonlight. Somewhere out there, Spit McGee was moving around in the moist Mississippi shadows, listening to the distant sounds of car motors idling in the road or girls squealing at each other on the Country Club veranda, chewing tobacco and feeling at home by himself. I wished I could warn him about the guns. We hadn't counted on *that*. But I knew he could take care of himself all right.

"Come on, Willie!" Rivers called.

"See you later, boys," I said and went to join her. Together we walked around the veranda that circled the fine old clubhouse. The main entrance to the ballroom was on the west side. Rivers proudly showed me the crepe streamers she'd helped put up, decorating the lofty French doors, and overhead a sign that she and Kay King and Margaret Pepper had painted:

YAZOO HIGH SENIOR PROM - '46

A fat girl wearing a blue gown that looked like the billowing sail on an ocean cruiser came up to us. It was Mary Jean Whitaker, the center on the girl's basketball team. She was holding something in the folds of her dress.

"What've you got there, Mary Jean?" I asked.

She revealed a small baseball bat with a blue ribbon tied around it that matched the color of her dress.

"Any devil worshipper tries to get his hands on me," Mary Jean said, "gets his head busted." Given the menacing girth of Mary Jean Whitaker, not to mention the beribboned baseball bat, even the most fanatic sacrificial killer would confront her at his risk.

"Well, don't take the bat with you onto the dance floor," I said. "Somebody might trip on it."

The band was warming up now, doing its grand riffs and scales, and the students packed the ballroom, waiting for the festive music to start. Furniture had been moved to make room for the dancing. The straight-backed chairs were lined up along the panelled walls, and streamers and balloons hung from the ceiling. Although this was my first Prom, I had an intuition the excitement tonight might be more effervescent than usual. Boys kept glancing around

102

defensively whenever somebody bumped into them. Girls shrieked at the slightest provocation, which is saying a great deal: Delta girls were born to shriek, as everybody who ever lived there knows. Here and there I saw older boys whispering among themselves, showing each other the items they carried inside their jackets or cumberbunds or back pockets. And it wasn't just flasks, either. I saw two switchblade knives, a homemade blackjack made from a sock full of BBs, and a slingshot with ball bearings for ammunition. We sprang from a society of histrionic drama, and everybody expected something to happen on this night. They were not going to be disappointed.

Rivers and I went inside and joined the party. We spoke to Mrs. Iris Dewberry, our English teacher, who wore so much makeup I hardly recognized her.If someone had jostled her, her nose might've fallen off. She was radiating some sort of perfume that would've awakened a swamp bear from profoundest hibernation.

She hugged Rivers as if she hadn't seen her in years and warned us not to go outside for *any reason*.

"Yes, ma'am," we said, and moved toward the bandstand.

The band had stopped warming up, and an expectant silence descended on the room. Then the lights were dimmed, and all of a sudden the Redtops exploded in their world-famous rendition of "The Sunny Side of the Street." The place went crazy. Rivers and I started dancing—I mean, our feet started dancing all by themselves—before we even touched hands. I guess it was in our blood. Everybody was jumping and gyrating, singing and dancing like mad. The Redtops were going like a musical locomotive and Yazoo High was aboard for the ride. For a while there was nothing but music, music, music, and we didn't have to do anything at all but dance. I saw Henjie jerking around with his date named Edna Crosswaite, and there was Bubba and Zamma Lou Bailey doing some kind of tango or carioca, and Billy stepping on Holly East's sensitive toes,

103

shorter by half a head than she was, leaping in the air as she turned under his arm or jumping high in his unlikely pirouettes.

We danced for a long time. When one song ended, another one began. After a while the Redtops took their first break, and Rivers and I went to the punch table and waited our turn in line.

"The devil worshippers are mostly after girls," Ann Marie Fitzsimmons, a senior cheerleader, told Rivers. "You be careful, honey."

"I'm not scared," another senior girl said. "Well, not much."

I got Rivers some fruit punch, and we stood around watching the older students. There was an electric air of agitation, like the cosmic static before a summer's thunderstorm. I couldn't help feeling that this Prom had something none of the previous ones had ever had, a palpable wild west quality–yet strangely Southern and Delta–of living on the dagger's edge of danger, when everyone went around *armed*. Had something been missing, before? Did Yazoo enjoy being terrified? There wasn't anybody in the place who didn't fully expect something to happen before the dance was over. Well, something was going to happen. It might not be the real thing, but it would be close to it. I mean, a person couldn't take a chance on the devil worshippers not coming out when they were supposed to, could he?

"Come on, Willie, let's dance!" Rivers said.

The Redtops had returned to the bandstand and were picking up their instruments. The drummer initiated a fast beat, and the piano and bass picked it up, and the saxophone and trumpet came in, and the singers grabbed their microphones and started to sing

When that deep purple falls
Over sleepy garden walls

and everybody began dancing at once all over again. I no-

104

ticed our own shadows leaping on the wall, bigger than life in their frisky silhouettes, as if Yazoo High had been transmuted into a cult of its own, jumping and stretching up our hands to worship—*what*? The Delta? Having whipped the Germans and Japanese? Being thirteen, or eighteen, or twelve and three quarters, and full of life's vibrant rhythms? It didn't really matter. We were like Casey Jones in our own county with a billowing head of steam. There was no stopping us now. It was the time of our time, and we would remember it.

About eleven o'clock the band took another intermission. The whole place was steaming now and everybody poured out onto the veranda. Despite the chaperones' instructions, students of all ages were walking around in clusters in the dark. Some of the senior boys congregated under a nearby water oak. Bubba came back from there and told me they were passing a bottle.

"What is it?" I said.

"It ain't Dr. Pepper," he said.

Rivers and I went to sit on the steps. Little streams of perspiration dripped softly from the familiar tiny cleft in her lip, the little cleft I'd known since our childhood. I couldn't help it. I leaned toward her and brushed the sweat from her lips with my fingers. She smiled, then giggled, then she just laughed at me, as if she were really having fun. Was she aware of the danger? Was I her knight in shining armor on this perilous, incipient night? Who was I? Who was she? What were we doing here? *Rivers*!

She and I drifted onto the second fairway, where other couples were casually walking up and down. Many of the older ones had their arms around each other. Rivers took off her shoes and walked in her stockings. The quarter moon was directly overhead, and stars flickered to the farthest horizon. The country club was like a brilliant island of light in a vast, twinkling ocean. Rivers' dress reflected that light and made her seem to glow in the dark.

I made up my mind I was going to do it. I was going to hold her hand. We bumped into each other now and then, comfortably, as we walked. Our hands were almost touching. What would she do? Would she let me? If she did, would it mean we were going steady? The girls in our class knew all the signs of romance. If you asked, they'd likely claim to have written the book of love itself. For example, according to them, in the seventh grade holding hands was next to being engaged. (What did you do at age 17, then?) However, we were seventh graders now, and holding hands was probably old hat. I had no way of knowing. Anyhow, the next time Rivers swung her arm gently between us, I opened my hand and caught hers in it. She didn't say a word. I held my breath. Then she began to swing my hand between us as we walked– like we had been holding hands all our lives–and I knew it was all right. Actually, it was so much better than all right there was no comparison.

"Look for a shooting star, Willie," Rivers said. "If you see one, make a wish."

"Okay," I said.

We'd reached the end of the fairway, near the bunkers under the green, when someone shouted, "*Look!*" There was a mad chorus of yells. We hurried to see what was happening. The others were gathered in the middle of the arched fairway, pointing out at something.

About two hundred yards away, on the sixth green— where I expected it to be–a circumference of light flickered and ebbed and sparkled and dazzled the eye against the encompassing night. The six lights which formed the circle seemed to wink on and off. Gradually it became apparent that the lights were actually flames. For a moment a heavy bizarre hush fell upon us, beginning with those of us gathered closely together there on the fairway and rippling down toward the clubhouse, as people became silent on the veranda, looking and pointing, and then on the lawn. I heard a policeman's leather belt and holster creaking as he desperately bolted toward us.

Spit had set the lights out nearly an hour before he was supposed to, I thought. He doesn't own a watch. The plan was for him to light them at midnight.

Then some of the senior boys began running toward the lights, giving an awesome high-pitched yell like charging Rebel cavalry. I believed I saw pistols and clubs and knives in some of their hands. One of them swung a baseball bat over his head. I told Rivers to stay right there and I took off after them. Suddenly there was an ever larger stampede among the spectators toward the mysterious palpitating lights. This was what they had been waiting for. It was like they *could* not wait, *would* not be denied. Girls held their pumps in their hands, hiked up their skirts and ran barefoot in the dew-wet grass, screaming as tradition itself dictated into the Delta dark. The faster boys got to the sixth green first, where they skidded to a precipitous halt. Now they saw that the lights were burning smudge pots (which Spit and I'd borrowed from a construction site on the edge of town), and then something else swiftly claimed their attention. A still form hung from the flagstaff marking the golf hole.

"What's *that*?" someone yelled.

"It's a baby!" another terrified voice shouted.

Screams of horror echoed across the green terrain. I was even a little horrified myself, even though I knew exactly what it was.

"No, it's a piece of cloth shaped like a baby," one of the senior boys said, and held up a blazing smudge pot so people could see. The crowd let out a collective gasp of relief.

I compressed my lips, stifling a big laugh that rose in me like a bubble.

"*There he goes!*" a boy yelled. "*Get him!*"

My frivolous amusement turned quickly to apprehension. I gazed out where people were pointing and saw a slender form scampering between the tight groves of trees. After he lit the smudge pots Spit was supposed to have taken off into the night. Obviously he had remained to enjoy what he had wrought.

A pistol cracked in the dark–a flat, evil sound, unlike the hollow ring of a firecracker–a deadly, purposeful pop. Girls squealed. Everybody ducked, then retreated helter skelter in every direction. A senior majorette ran into me and nearly knocked me down. I recovered my balance and dashed in the direction of the pack of angry boys pursuing Spit. I mightn't have caught them if the one with the pistol–it was Bobby Shoemaker–hadn't stopped to take aim. As I ran desperately toward him, I caught a fleeting glimpse of Spit struggling to climb a rise. No one else recognized him, but even at a distance of thirty or so yards I made out his fishing cap with the lures attached to it bobbing up and down as he scaled a bunker and was briefly, perilously outlined against the starry sky–a clear target if ever there was one.

I reached Bobby Shoemaker just before he pulled the trigger. I lowered my shoulder and hit him in the side of the legs with a perfect body block that hurt like hell. Me, that is. I must've bounced off him, because the next thing I knew, he'd grabbed my collar and stubbornly jerked me to my feet.

"*Excuse me!*" I yelled. From afar I heard people laughing.

"Who is it?" he demanded, pulling my face close to his so he could identify me in the dark. "Are you Willie Morris?"

"Yes it is!" I said dizzily.

"What're you tryin' to do?"

"I bumped into you in the dark, is all," I said.

"You nearly broke my leg."

"I'm sorry."

"Well, it's a lucky thing you ran into a good guy, or you might've got the devil beat out of you, boy."

Just then Sheriff Biggers came trotting up to us, gasping hard for breath. He shined his flashlight on us. "Who fired that shot?" he demanded. Then he saw the pistol in Bobby's hand. "Give me that piece, son, handle first." Bobby meekly obeyed. "You got a license for that?" Bobby shook his head. "I thought so," the sheriff said. "All right. You come with me while I look around. You're gonna have to go to the station with me in a minute, soon as we get this settled."

Everybody stood around dubiously while the sheriff shined his flashlight on the bunker and searched for the culprit, who by now had to have been very far away, beyond the hills and into the woods. The sheriff returned and announced that whoever it was had escaped into the dense foliage bordering the club property. Several of the older boys wanted to form a posse and look for, as one of their number said, the "devil worshipping son of a gun," but the sheriff ordered them to go on home, that he and his men would scour the woods for any signs of tracks first thing in the morning.

I tried hard to convince myself that this was what I had in mind all along, to get people involved in the positive act of searching the county for the genuine felons, instead of sitting around gossiping all the time and doing nothing. I had to tell myself twice, however, before I began to believe it.

"Is that Willie Morris?" the sheriff said, when someone pointed me out and reported to him what I'd done. "You have a way of bein' where the action is, boy." In the dark I could feel the senior boys looking at me with a grudging respect. To be honest I wasn't too unproud of myself, either.

The crowd mindlessly started to leave. Rivers found me and grabbed hold of my hand, right there in front of the sheriff and everybody.

"You were so brave," she said. "If you hadn't stopped him from shooting, someone might've been hurt."

109

"Yep," I said, like Gary Cooper in *Sergeant York*.

Back at the clubhouse, the chaperones were adamant for closing down the Prom, but the seniors begged them to let the Redtops play "Danny Boy," which was always their next to the last number. Some of the senior girls took Rivers and me to stand up front with the graduating class, the Yazoo Class of '46, in the place of honor near the band. When the Redtops began to sing, everybody linked arms and swayed slowly back and forth.

Oh Danny Boy, the pipes, the pipes are calling,
From glen to glen and down the mountainside,
The summer's gone and all the roses falling,
It's you, it's you must go and I must bide.

Girls were bawling, and even some of the big old boys were struggling to keep from crying, too. And they'd never cried until now. Rivers held my hand tightly. Everybody was singing now. I didn't know all the lyrics of the song, but whatever words I sang were close enough. I wouldn't have wanted Spit McGee to get killed, having provided a fine moment like this, of course, but if he'd gotten hit, a flesh wound wouldn't really have been so bad. After all, it was only a .22.

110

Twelve

RIVERS WAS HOLDING ME close and kissing my cheek which was wet with tears as I tenderly sang "Danny Boy." Then she was kissing the corner of my mouth. Then I turned toward her and...

I woke up with Skip licking my face. I looked at the alarm clock on my dresser. It was 9:05 a.m. and Skip wanted to be let out. I rose and went down the hall to the back door. Skip danced and pranced until I got the door open and he zipped out into the fresh free glow of Saturday.

"Willie, is that you?" Mama called from the kitchen. "Come tell me about last night."

Although she'd been waiting up for me the night before and had interrogated me about the Prom while I undressed to go to bed, I hadn't deigned to tell her about the melodramatic incident on the golf course. Now I had a feeling she'd already been on the phone with some of her friends and knew the whole story. Yawning, I went into the kitchen and sat down at the table. Mama brought me some orange juice and sat across from me, waiting. I drank the whole glass very slowly. Mama was very pretty, as I've already suggested, for a long-armed woman with a comb, but I hated her wrinkled brow when she was worried about me. It made her look older than she was, and I was the last to want Mama to grow old. Although she sometimes drove me crazy with things, I really wished she'd live forever, but I never once told her that. How to understand these things of the heart?

"What's for breakfast?" I said.

"Cheerios," Mama said.

"What else is there?"

"You like Cheerios," she said, waving her hand in a tiny impatient arc. She brought me a bowl and a spoon, cereal and milk. "Well?" she prompted.

"We had a great time," I said, dumping the cereal in the bowl and sprinkling some sugar on it, then pouring the milk. Mama waited some more. I started eating.

"And?" she said.

"You know, we danced and sang and stuff."

"What else?"

"Nothing much. Oh," I took another bite, "somebody lit some smudge pots on the golf course."

"Uh-huh!" she said. "You make it sound like they were paving the parking lot. William Weaks Morris, don't you sit there and pretend that nothing happened. The devil worshippers made a circle of fire around a sacrificial victim and people were scared to death. You were right in the middle of it, and there was shooting. You could've been *killed!*" Mama's voice rose to a frantic impetuous little shriek, like the girls the night before. I knew from experience she'd turn up the volume any minute.

"Bobby Shoemaker fired a pistol into the woods," I said calmly. "That's all. There was no 'sacrificial victim.' Nobody got hurt. It was no big deal."

"That's not the way I heard it!" she said. "I wanted your

father to have a serious talk with you this morning, but he had to go to work at the station. He'll see you this evening when he gets home. Do you hear?"

"Yes, ma'am."

That was all right with me. Daddy would figure out what he wanted to say to me and by the time he got around to it, the situation would've cooled down to the point of old history. The truth was, he probably was proud of me for doing what I did. Half the people in town had bragged on me last night. Bobby Shoemaker even shook hands with me later and said he was glad he hadn't shot anybody, after all.

"And I want you to go see your grandfather," Mama said. "You haven't see him all week."

"Yes, ma'am."

The phone rang and Mama rushed into the hall to answer it. She looked disappointed when she returned to the kitchen and said it was Bubba. I finished the last of my Cheerios and went to the phone.

"Hey, Bubba," I said.

"Are you listenin' to the radio?" he said excitedly.

"No." I was instantly on guard. This was what we said to people when we phoned to tell them they were on the air and would win a trip to Hollywood if they could correctly answer a radio quiz question.

"This ain't no joke, Willie," he said. "They caught one of the devil worshippers. Turn on your radio. It's on WAZF, right now!"

I hung up without saying goodbye and hastened to the living room to turn on our Philco. I stood there tapping my fingers on the wooden console, waiting for the radio to warm up. Finally it came on. I tuned our local station, WAZF, just in time to hear the announcer:

"...and Mayor Stokes has called a town meeting at two o'clock this afternoon at the courthouse concerning the alleged sacrificial devil worship in Yazoo County. At the

113

meeting a self-confessed demonologist, as yet unidentified, is expected to come forward and testify. The public is urged to attend."

I stood there dumbstruck while the announcer ran an advertisement: "Jones' Feed and Seed Store is your Yazoo headquarters for farm and garden supplies. We got the best prices in town. We got everything. Come get your fertilizer now. Remember, Jones' is where the elite meet for feed and seed…"

It seemed impossible that a real demonologist had been unmasked. In all this time I'd never actually envisioned what they might look like. In my mind's emotion they'd remained saturnine, faceless personages dancing around a fire, wearing devil masks and chanting things, with murder in their lungs. Had one of them actually been arrested? The lieutenant from the Mississippi Bureau of Investigation had told the townspeople that such practices weren't against the law. How had it happened? Had he, or she, simply given up? It didn't seem fair, somehow, for them to quit on us when we least expected it.

I went to my room and started getting dressed. I knew one thing: it wouldn't be easy to wait until 2 p.m.

In the meantime I went to see my granddaddy Percy.

I loved Percy more than anything. He was my best friend. I know that's a strange thing to say about your grandfather, but it was true. Percy and I got along like biscuits and molasses or rice and gravy. He knew how to make things out of nothing, like bass plugs and bird calls and flutes. He knew where the prime fishing holes were. He liked the good things of life, like baseball and fried goggle-eye and moonpies and Errol Flynn movies. There wasn't anything I couldn't ask Percy about. Today, however, I was a little nervous about what he might ask *me*. Percy knew me better than anybody, better maybe than I knew myself.

I found him in his workroom in the old barn behind his house. On his worktable was a model of the famous steamship, The Delta Queen, built to scale. He was carefully whittling some little wooden part to go on it. He didn't pay me much attention at first. I sidled up and watched over his shoulder.

"The Delta Queen's looking good, Percy," I said.

"Thanks, Willie," he said, and kept on whittling. "How was the dance?"

"It was just fine."

"I can't make much sense of the way kids dance these days. Guess I'm old-fashioned."

"What's that piece you're working on?"

"It's one of the struts that support the roof of the pilot house. Let's see, now. I've got it the right size. All it needs is a little glue at each end..." He dipped the stick into a glue bottle. "...And it goes right here. How's that?"

I watched him fit the miniature strut into place.

"That's perfect," I said.

"You want to do the next one?" he said.

"Sure."

He gave me his knife and a little piece of wood and watched closely as I tried to carve out a strut as I'd seen him do.

"Mind that knife," he said. "It's awful sharp."

"How'm I doing?"

"Shave a little more off the bottom." Percy drew back and regarded me as I worked. I could feel a lecture coming, which he seldom did. "You're growin' up mighty fast, Willie," he began.

"Um-hmm," I said.

"At your age, things can change so fast a young man hardly knows which end's up sometimes."

"Um-hmm."

"One thing won't change, though. You're a good boy, Willie. You wouldn't ever do anything to hurt anybody."

"No, sir," I said, continuing to whittle while listening to what he was saying.

115

"You do like to play a joke, though. Well, so do I. It's just—well, don't let a joke get out of hand."

I knew what he was talking about, and I appreciated the quiet way he went about it.

"I won't Percy," I said. "Well, it's ready."

"All right, put some glue on it," he said.

I dipped the stick in the glue bottle and fitted the tiny strut into place beside the other one. "How's that?" I said.

"Looks real good."

"Well, I gotta go now," I said.

"All right, Willie. Come back tomorrow and we'll get us a moonpie and an R.C."

"Thanks, Percy," I said.

"I'm here if you need to talk—you know that?"

"Yessir."

"You be careful now."

"Yessir, Percy."

As I left the barn and headed to Bubba's house I contemplated his words: *Don't let it get out of hand.* But I had a nagging feeling it already had.

I was one of the fortunate few who got a seat in the court-room. Bubba, Henjie, Billy and I'd been waiting outside the courthouse since after lunch. I would've skipped lunch, to make sure we got inside, but Bubba said he'd starve to death if he didn't get something to eat first. We'd gone to Bubba's for lunch. Bubba's mother gave us hot dogs and potato chips, and Cokes and chocolate chip cookies, which we gulped down and thanked her for while going out the door. Bubba only had time to eat three hot dogs, and he complained all the way to the Courthouse.

We split up, so that Bubba and I sat together on the third row while Henjie and Billy were toward the back. People were standing in the aisles and sitting in the jury box. There must've been nearly four hundred people crowded into a room built for about half that many.

116

The mayor entered from the judge's chambers. With him were the sheriff and the lieutenant from the capital city. They took their places behind the law clerk's long mahogany table in front. The mayor stood up and the room got quiet.

"I'd like to call this meeting to order," he said. "Well, I hate to say I told you so, but this witch hunt business got way out of hand. Too much false information going around and too much talk. If folks had shown more faith in their law enforcement officials, the problem wouldn't have arisen. Your sheriff's department didn't panic, however. No sir! With the result that we're now in a position to lay this witch business to rest. We have an individual here today who can shed light on the situation. This individual, I might add, has been forthcoming of his own volition. I think you'll be very interested in what he has to say. Now I'll call on him to come forward. –Mr. Sledge?"

A grievous hush fell over the room, then the crowd made a collective *ohhhhh* as a pale, slender man with a beakish nose got up and made his way to the front. A woman on the row in front of me sat on the edge of her seat, blocking my vision. I stood up to see, and a man behind me said, "Down in front!" I sat back down and leaned this way and that, trying to get an unencumbered view. Then the man named Sledge stepped up on the raised dais, and the mayor gestured for him to stand at the podium.

He faced the audience. I could hardly believe my eyes. Was this pint-sized, skinny-necked, pale-faced, middle-aged, mostly bald-headed man in his plain black suit, white shirt and striped tie and thick, hornrimmed glasses over his auspicious nose the one everyone had been so terrified of? He looked as innocuous as a tadpole. If a devil-worshipper had to come forward, I thought irritably, he might at least have looked the part.

"My name is Irwin Sledge," the man said, speaking so low I could barely hear him even sitting near the front.

117

"*What?*" some people near the back called. "Speak up! We can't hear you."

"My name is Sledge," the man repeated. "I'm from Belzoni."

"What did he say?" about fifty people buzzed at once.

"*Sledge!*" the man cried. "*From Belzoni.*"

"Okay, we hear you now," someone yelled from the back. An uneasy titter of laughter ran through the packed chamber.

"I been engaged in witchcraft activity for eight years." Women gasped as Sledge of Belzoni hurried on. "That's not as bad as it sounds. The fact is, me and my friends don't actually *worship* the devil or nothin'. We just get together at night in our pickup trucks, somewhere in the county, and enjoy each other's company."

"Doin' *what?*" somebody yelled from the back of the room. The same restless laughter rippled from the audience again.

"Meetin' unusual people and gettin' acquainted," Sledge explained, obviously warming to the attention.

"Can you be more specific?" the mayor interrupted. "You know, what you told us."

"We dress up in devil costumes mostly for the fun of it." The man seemed to solicit the audience's sympathy. "There's not much goin' on in Belzoni at night, you know. Things are pretty dead over there. If you don't believe it, come see for yourself. Jackson's a long drive to find somethin' to do on Saturday night. Ain't nothin' goin' on in Indianola or Midnight, I can tell you. Or in Hollandale neither. So it just sort of happened that a group of us started meetin' at this gravel pit in Yazoo County and parked our pickups in a circle and, you know, just hung out together. We didn't, to my knowledge, break any laws."

The disappointment in the room was almost tangible. After all the rumors, the panic, the dead crow on the witch's grave, the burning cross at Miss Eddie Mack's, the telephone calls, the children kept home from school, the run on pistols at Lucky Dan's Pawn Shop, girls in evening gowns carrying baseball bats, Bobby Shoemaker with a pistol under his cumberbund, here was one Irwin Sledge of Belzoni suggesting that our great witch's scare was nothing but a group of bored, lonely, paltry people meeting in a gravel pit? What a letdown!

"What about the phone calls to the pet shop about buyin' animals for sacrifice?" a woman in the audience asked Sledge.

"It wasn't me," he said.

"What about the signs written in blood?" someone said. "What about them Latin words?"

"No, that wasn't me, neither," he declared. "I don't know no Latin."

"Did you kill animals?" a man asked.

"Not unless we was goin' to have a barbeque," Sledge said earnestly. An immense laugh went up. Sledge smiled. He was really enjoying being the center of attention now. "We had a Hawaiian luau party once and butchered a pig. I got the recipe for the sauce if anybody's interested."

"Was it extra hot?" a man yelled.

This brought the house down. It was nearly two minutes before the mayor could restore order. The candid outlander waited patiently for things to quieten down.

Then someone asked: "If it wasn't you or your fellow night owls from the gravel pit that made those bloody signs and put dead crows all around Yazoo, then who did? That's what I want to know."

The courtroom grew very still. The pause was tense now.

"I don't know," Mr. Sledge said, "but I wouldn't be surprised if it was just some practical joker. There's a lot of copy-cattin' going on. It gives a bad name to the serious practitioners of witchcraft, the ones in California who write articles and put on seminars and conferences about the occult every Halloween. I even subscribe to one of their papers, called *The Devil's Advocate*. But that practical joker of yours might be in this very room."

Now people began to glance around suspiciously. I saw a woman staring at Bubba and me, and glancing aside I realized what she was looking at: Bubba's face had turned beet red—not just a regular blush but a deep crimson that was like a neon sign saying: *guilty, guilty, guilty.*

Lucky for us, the mayor chose that moment to take charge again of the meeting. The audience turned its fractious attention to the speaker's table, while the mayor thanked Mr. Sledge for coming forward. Then he addressed the crowd.

"If the pranks continue," he said, "and that's all they really are—just pranks—we'll catch who's doing it. In the meantime, let's stop talking, let's stop letting our imaginations run wild, let's calm down and get on with our daily routines. Let's just make money and raise our crops and go to church and love our little children. I officially declare this silly witch scare *over and done with!*"

A cheer went up, and the audience happily disbursed, talking and laughing about Mr. Irwin Sledge and pickup trucks and demons' wardrobes and Hawaiian luaus with extra hot sauce and how dull it must be in Belzoni at night. Bubba scrambled out of the courtroom like a rooftop thief, followed by Henjie and Billy who looked none too innocent themselves. I was going to have to talk to them. As I went up the aisle I noticed Mr. Sledge standing by himself, waiting for the crowd to thin before he left. I mean, after a confession like Sledge's, nobody exactly rushed up to get his autograph, especially in a neighborhood of diligent church-goers.

One question burned on my mind, however, and I couldn't resist going up to him.

"Excuse me, sir," I said, "could you tell me the location of the gravel pit you mentioned?"

"You look a bit young for our group," he said.

120

"I just wanted to know where it is, that's all."

He looked me over. Then he must've realized he was in no position to make righteous and threatening judgments of anybody, not after his own pallid confessional. "It's north of the farm-to-market road that crosses the county line near Yellow Creek."

That didn't mean much to me because I'd never been there. I asked him if his group had ever parked anywhere near the Yazoo garbage dump, meaning the place Ollie had shown me.

"A garbage dump?" Sledge said indignantly. "What do you take me for, a buzzard?"

I noticed the lieutenant from the Bureau of Investigation looking quizzically at me, so I turned abruptly and went up the aisle. What Mr. Sledge had said direly troubled me. Ollie had shown me the bloody feathers, the burnt logs, the shredded bones, the black candle stubs which were patent evidence that devil worshippers had been there—or someone who wanted people to think they were devil worshippers. It was clear to me that regardless of the visitor's story, many perplexing and unanswered questions remained. If the authorities weren't going to find the answers, someone else had to. This case was far from closed.

At this recognition my spirits lifted and I went outside looking for my friends. They were standing under a pecan tree in front of the courthouse near the iron benches where the farmers congregated when they came into town on Saturday.

"Bubba," I said, "your face is your own worst enemy."

"What, are my ears too big?" he said selfconsciously.

"No, I mean the way you turned red in there."

Ordinarily Henjie and Billy would've laughed at Bubba's expense. Now they just gazed away with solemn expressions as if neither of them wanted to look me straight in the eye. Something was wrong.

"Listen," I said, "this case isn't over. That Sledge person's

121

not the same one who burned the cross in Miss Eddie Mack's front yard and everything. Somebody *else* did it. Listen to me!"

"No, Willie," Bubba said, "you listen. We're tired of your game. We've had enough."

"*My* game!" I said.

"It ain't fun no more," Henjie said. "We want out."

"Yeah," Billy chimed in. "*Out!*"

"Did you hear what Sledge said!" I exclaimed. "His group met at a gravel pit on the county line. That's the wrong place."

"*This* is the wrong place," Bubba whispered. I followed his sharp warning glance and saw the sheriff at a courthouse window. He was staring down at us. "We're gettin' out before you get us into any more trouble," he added. "You're real trouble, Willie." He started indignantly walking away, and Billy and Henjie immediately fell in behind him.

"Get out before it's too late," Bubba called over his shoulder.

"Yeah, bail out!" Henjie said.

"Hey, I thought you were good old boys!" I called lamely after them. But I had already lost them, irrevocably and forever.

Bubba had been right about one thing, though. People were watching us. The mayor had called on the community to seek out the "culprits," hadn't he? I could feel unknown eyes following me as I walked down the sidewalk. I began whistling the Yazoo fight song. When I came to the first corner, I turned it and ran like the dickens.

Thirteen

I DIDN'T SLOW DOWN until I reached the field west of town
where we played our baseball. I kicked at rusty tin cans
and sticks and dirt clods, threw rocks at some gracklings
in a chinaberry tree. *Think*, Miss Eddie Mack had said. For
the first time in weeks I really tried to use my God-given
head. What a fool I was!

I had the definite feeling people were sorry the witch
scare was over, though few of them of course would admit
it. All the mystery and excitement had been like a lush
spring rain in a drought of dreadful ennui and boredom.
During the war everybody blacked out their windows, but
had the Luftwaffe bombed Yazoo? No. They never even
went after the sawmill. Nothing ever happened here. An
occasional robbery or car wreck or the Clyde Beatty Circus
with its skinny tigers, the cruel whips lashing at the poor
tigers' backs so that I felt sorry for them—that's about all—
barely worth a paragraph in the Jackson *Clarion-Ledger*.
That's why there was so much commotion over the witch

hunt. But if I could figure that out, somebody else could, too. I was lonesome.

"Who you talkin' to, Willie?" a voice said. "Just yo'self?"

I looked up, and there stood Ollie grinning at me. I hadn't noticed him sneaking up on me.

"Nobody," I said, and kicked at another can. Ollie instantly absorbed my mood. He pretended to admire the distance the can traveled, as if I were drop-kicking field goals.

"Wanta play some ball?" he suggested.

"Not right now."

He fell in beside me. I continued kicking the can and we followed its random, zigzag path across the field. When we came to the woods, he lightly touched my shoulder with his hand.

"Want to see sump'm?" he said.

"What?"

"There's another place like the one I showed you."

"Where!"

"It's farther out than the other one. But it's got the same tire tracks and stacked logs and ashes on the ground and chicken feathers and animal hides—and bones."

"*Let's go!*" I yelled.

This time we followed a winding dirt trail that sliced headlong through the woods beyond the river. Then it abruptly came out on a red clay road that twisted along a great, gullied ridge. At the tallest point there was a break in the treeline, and we could see the rooftops of the town, and the high cupola of the courthouse, and the train depot, all the hidden glimpses of the funny old town so long ago, but we didn't take time to stop and enjoy the view. Farther down the trail resumed on the other side of the dirt road, and we entered the dark, enshrouded woods again. After what seemed hours—but was probably little more than thirty minutes—we came back to the same secret road. At least Ollie said it was the same road. I couldn't tell. It turned into a two-rut lane that eventually dead-ended in tall slender timber on someone's property line bordered by a high, rusty barbed wire fence. We climbed over it and followed a cow path into the pines. Way back in the middle of nowhere, Ollie led me into a melancholy hidden glade where we came suddenly upon a fire-blackened pit with stacked logs. Bloody feathers and animal skins were scattered all around, along with the inevitable black candle stubs, and strange leg bones with dry sinews of flesh. What struck me at once was the similarity to the first site he'd shown me. Something seemed artificial and contrived about the identical pattern of this grotesque disarray.

And something more: There was a routine, workmanlike quality in the scattered debris. There was method in somebody's madness. Whoever had been here seemed intent on making the site look like a place where men sacrificed beasts. If evil had been present here it was of a different kind, methodical and sham and regimented.

"Look at that pit," I pointed. "Why would they dig it so deep and square off the corners?"

"Maybe they used it for a cook-fire," Ollie said.

"To cook food?"

"Maybe they cooked mash," he said.

"What's mash?"

"You know, corn and barley oats—what they makes moonshine out of."

I gave Ollie a wild look of amazement.

"Ollie, you're a genius!" My exaggerated shout resounded through the silent pines.

"What did I say?" he asked.

"Come on!" I said. "We gotta get back to town. I gotta tell the sheriff..."

"Whoa, not me!" Ollie frowned. "I ain't tellin' no sheriff nothin'."

"But we got proof," I insisted.

"Proof nothin'. You gonna git yourself a whole lotta trouble if you don't look out." He began backing away.

125

"You goin' back to town with me?" I said.

"Uh-uh," he said, shaking his head back and forth, then gazing at me with untrusting eyes. "I druther not be seen with you for awhile, Willie. I'll see you *later*."

And with that he turned and vanished forthwith into the trees. I retraced our path through the woods and found the two-rut road beyond the barbed wire fence, but there was no sign of Ollie. All the way back into town I kept thinking, This is *it*.

I was pretty hot and tired by the time I reached the sheriff's office, which was in the old red-brick jail, about two blocks from the Courthouse. I went into the foyer and loitered around for a minute or so looking at the Wanted posters. This was one of those places—which included the Clark Mansion, the cemetery and, until recently, Miss Eddie Mack's house—that I tended to avoid. After a while, however, I made my mind up and steeled myself and went inside.

Although I'd never been in the sheriff's office before, the low enclosed ceiling and plastered walls painted dull military green and the close smell of tobacco and sweat seemed somehow familiar. Had I been here in my dreams? A hardfaced woman in a police uniform with funny wispy lip whiskers for a female sat before a formidable counter. She was reading a movie magazine. Behind her was a radio set with earphones and a microphone. Even her nose looked mean. She reminded me of the Nazi S.S. women in the war movies, pasty-faced and very sadistic, the ones who tortured little children with lighted cigarettes and pried toenails off people and enjoyed watching them beg and
cry and squirm.

"Who are *you*?" she said, looking up impatiently.

"I want to see the sheriff."

"That ain't what I said. Who are you?"

"Willie Morris."

"Oh!" She seemed surprised. Then she yelled into another room, "Sheriff? The Morris boy's come to turn hisself in, the sorry little bugger."

"*Turn myself in?*" I said.

I heard the leather holster creak and thudding footsteps coming to the door. Then Sheriff Biggers loomed in the doorway, big as Paul Bunyan, big as the law itself, big as the cruelest retribution.

"I want to talk to you," he said.

He took me into his office. There, to my astonished disbelief, sat Bubba, Billy and Henjie. One look at their guilty expressions told me what had happened: *they had ratted.*

Around the room, with faces of stone, like Mount Rushmore come to Yazoo, were our parents, Principal Barnes, Mrs. Martin the librarian, Miss Abbott, and Lieutenant McDowell from the capital city. Their silence was appalling. My mother looked on the dim edge of tears, my daddy hurt and embarrassed. I'd let them down. Seeing Daddy so sad made me feel terrible, the worst I'd ever felt in my life. My legs were clumsily shaking. I locked my knees to keep anyone from noticing.

"Well, Willie," the sheriff said, "what've you got to say for yourself?"

"I got evidence..." I said, fumbling in my pocket for the candle stub.

"So do we, Willie Morris!" Miss Abbott broke in fiercely. "My neighbor saw you sneaking across my yard..."

"I remembered you asking about that book on witchcraft, Willie," said Mrs. Martin.

"He was asking questions at our school assembly," Mr. Barnes said.

"Willie, were you not at Miss Eddie Mack's the night the cross was burned?" the sheriff demanded. "And what about the Prom? Did you steal those smudge pots?"

"Tell the truth," Mr. Barnes said. "Did you tie that crow to the flagpole?"

"Well, not exactly," I muttered, looking despairingly from face to face.

"Tell the truth, boy!" the sheriff ordered.

"Sheriff, I've got important information about the devil worshippers," I said in a torrid rush. "They may be connected with the moonshiners the lieutenant told us about." I glanced hopefully at the state investigator. He seemed interested, but before I could continue the sheriff interrupted.

"We got some serious charges against you, boy," he said. "Stealin' city property, breakin' and enterin', defacin' public monuments, killin' a crow without a huntin' license, vandalism, disturbin' the peace. I want to know who your accomplice was, the night of the Prom. It'll go harder on you if you don't tell. Was it Spit McGee? These boys said he was hangin' around the Clark Mansion a week ago Friday when y'all painted that sign. Was it Spit? The principal tells me he's been absent from school."

"I'm sorry, but I can't tell you that, sir," I said.

"Why not?"

"It's a matter of honor."

"*Honor!*" Miss Abbott burst out. She was about to say something else, but my mother suddenly glared at her, twisting her eyes at her in a bitter glare. I felt a little better, knowing Mama hadn't completely disowned me.

"Willie," Mr. Barnes said, "You're a good boy with a fine record. Go on and tell the sheriff what he wants to know."

"Yessir," I said, "but those places in the woods I found oughta be investigated." I put the black candle stub on the sheriff's desk. "One of them's back behind the city dump. The other's about three miles from town where Ridge Road dead-ends. Someone's covering up..."

The sheriff rudely tossed the black candle stub into his trash can and laughed. He guffawed so hard his belly shook. "Someone's coverin' somethin' up, all right," he said, "and we know who he is. Son, you're in this up to your ears. It'll go easier on you if you tell us about it."

I looked from face to face. Everybody, my parents and teachers and friends, were waiting for me to do the right thing. There was a frog in my throat. I swallowed hard and said, "I'm sorry. We were just havin' some fun. I didn't kill that crow. It was already dead."

Fourteen

IN PUNISHING US, THE sheriff and our parents gave us the worst possible penalty on the Lord's earth. After all, Mississippi law in 1946 only went as far as the death penalty. We were sentenced to *Summer School.*

The next afternoon I was sitting under the elm tree in my backyard chewing on a grass stem. My baseball glove was lying on the ground beside me, but there wasn't any point in throwing flies in the air to myself. With all the practice time I'd lose, I probably wouldn't even make the team. The only worse thing would be if Miss Abbott was our Summer School teacher. I was a convicted criminal. I didn't care if I ever saw anybody again. I felt both guilty and betrayed, but what I really felt was awful.

I didn't hear my granddaddy Percy come up.

"Hello, Willie," he said, squatting beside me.

"Oh, hey, Percy."

"Thought you might need a little company just now." He

thoughtfully looked off into the woods back behind our house.

"Thanks, but I'd just as soon be by myself right now," I said, then remembered that I hadn't seen Skip all day. "Percy, you haven't seen Old Skip, have you?"

"He's probably off chasin' squirrels," Percy said. "He'll be back."

I glanced sideways at him. "You don't hate me, do you?" I said. "If *you* hate me..."

Percy plucked himself a long blade of grass to chew. "Of course not, boy. Your Mama and Daddy and I are concerned about you, that's all. We want you to be all right. Growin' up's not always easy. Sometimes things have a way of gettin' out of hand, like I said. Lots of juices flowin' inside. People are kinda mean to others, but they forget—they got their own problems sooner or later. But if a fella has a good heart—like you do—and puts a good face on his troubles, he'll come through all right."

"You think so?"

"I know so." Percy grinned and reached into his coat pocket. "I noticed that old baseball of yours was gettin' pretty banged up and..." He produced a brand new Spalding baseball with a Ted Williams autograph printed on it.

"*Wow!*" I said. "Thanks, Percy."

Just then, my daddy came out of the house carrying my fungo bat.

"Come on, Willie," Daddy yelled. "I'll hit you a few flies while your Mama cooks supper."

I saw Mama standing behind the screen door looking at Percy and me.

"We're havin' your favorite, Willie!" she called to me. "Pork chops and mashed potatoes and gravy."

I jumped up and grabbed my glove and ran on out to the vacant lot beyond the house. I didn't want them to see me crying.

131

"Look sharp, Willie," Daddy called. "Here comes a bases-loaded double!"

After supper I went out looking for Skip. I rode my bike all over town, calling and whistling for him everywhere. Several times I saw people turn away from me. Mr. Josephs, who owned the dry cleaners next to my daddy's filling station, was mowing his yard, and he keep mowing right around the corner of the house so he wouldn't have to speak to me. Mrs. Stembridge, the court reporter, was walking down the sidewalk and turned her head away when she saw me. I just kept riding and calling. I could hear my own mournful echo off the distant facades of the familiar old houses and buildings: *"Old Skip, where are you?"*

I rode everywhere that Skip usually went when he made his rounds. There was a boxer puppy on Main Street that he liked to visit. And a Scottish terrier that he fooled around with on Calhoun Avenue. And a big, shaggy dog–part Lab, part Saint Bernard–that Skip looked up to on Jefferson Street. And a hybrid old hound that I knew he admired. I half-expected to see Old Skip coming out of somebody's yard, jumping through the bushes when he heard me whistling. But he didn't.

I rode until dark–an hour after dark–before I gave up. I put my bike in our garage and sat on the front steps until bedtime, waiting for Skip. He rarely stayed out all night, but on the three or four times he had, he was waiting on the back steps for me to let him in, first thing in the morning.

Just before I went to bed exhausted, I was sitting in the kitchen with my head in my hands on the table. Suddenly Mama came out in her nightgown. I felt her put her hands around my head and hug me. She didn't have the comb for my cowlick now. She kissed me on the forehead. I really felt like a little boy now. I couldn't help it. "Where's Skip,

132

Mama?" She hugged me and kissed me again. "He'll be back, son."

It felt strange and empty to go to sleep without Skip warming the foot of my bed. I was used to pushing him out of the way so I could turn over. That night the bed seemed too big for me. It was hard to go to sleep. Just when I was in that hazy, half-awake, half-asleep state, I thought of the devil worshippers and sat up in bed, staring at the wall. Then something struck me.

Had they taken Skip?

I tossed and turned all night, sitting up every time I heard a noise, hoping it was Skip scratching at the door to be let in. At first light I went to the back door and looked out. He wasn't there. I got dressed and took my baseball glove and sat on the steps pounding the pocket of the glove. I heard Mama stirring around in the kitchen and went inside.

She fixed bacon and eggs and toast, but I wasn't hungry. I pretended to eat, moving the food around on my plate with my fork, and then went outside to look for Skip some more. In the back of my mind the nightmare kept coming back, looming unfocused like the blackest cloud: where was he? Did *they* have him?

I got on my bike and rode around town again, whistling for him everywhere. Without paying particular attention to where I was going, I rode up Witch's Hill, where Miss Eddie Mack lived. Something drew me to the lopsided little compound of roofed walkways and outbuildings behind the high privet hedge and secret little mewses. I parked my bike and went to knock on the door.

"Who is it?" Miss Eddie Mack called from inside.

"It's me, Willie," I said.

The door opened and she stood there smiling at me. She was wearing black mechanic's overalls and a man's straw hat, her hair sticking out from under it like grey wires.

"Have you seen my dog Skip?" I said.

133

"No. Is he missing? Come in, Willie."

She took me into her kitchen and told me to sit at the table while she made her herbal tea. I didn't especially want any, but I didn't refuse either. I told her about Skip—and everything else that had happened in the last two days. Things poured out.

"Don't you worry," she said at last, blowing on her tea and taking a delicate first sip. "We'll find your dog, and as for the other problem—well, time will take care of that. Folks will forget the whole thing. You'll see. People always have their own problems to think about sooner or later. They just turn on people because they're worried about their own selves." She sounded just like Percy.

"Yes, ma'am," I sighed, thinking of three months of summer school stretching from here to infinity. "Well, where else can I look for Skip? I've already searched every place I can think of."

She sipped her tea and looked at me steadily over the rim of her cup.

"I reckon I know where they've taken the dog," she said.

"*Ma'am?*" I nearly dropped my teacup, and immediately set it on the table.

"You guessed right," she went on. "I hate to say it, but the ones that's been causing all the trouble probably snatched your dog. They want to make an example of you, make it look like you've got some definite connection with the so-called 'witches,' and keep fear alive in this town."

"Who *are* they?" I was scared right down to my toes at the idea of faceless, enigmatic men holding Skip captive. Was he tied to a stake with his tail between his legs?

"You'll know directly," she said mysteriously. "Come on. We've got some traveling to do."

Numbed by Miss Eddie Mack's businesslike manner and the fact that she seemed to know who *they* were, I followed her through the house. We descended the roofed walkway leading to her tool shed. Since she obviously didn't own a

134

car, I wondered how we were going to go anywhere. Then she pulled the tarpaulin off a bulky object in a corner of the shed, and there was a red motorscooter.

It was a Cushman Flyer with small, thick rubber wheels and big metal fenders with storage compartments in them and a passenger seat behind the driver. I stared at it enviously.

"It runs like a top," she said proudly. "I do all the mechanical work myself."

"I never saw you riding it around town," I said.

"The only time I ride it is late at night. If the ladies of Yazoo saw me blasting up Grand Avenue on this machine, they'd take it as a direct assault on Southern womanhood."

"Are we going to wait until dark to go looking for Skip?" I said.

"Nope," she replied. "Today I'm going to make my motorscooter debut in Yazoo in broad daylight."

She examined the gas tank, tilted the scooter and kicked back the metal kickstand, then wheeled the machine smartly around and out through the door into the yard. Giving the hand throttle a couple of twists, she stomped on the starter pedal and the engine roared to life. The muffler must've been worn out, because when she raced the engine it was so loud she couldn't hear me shouting into her ear:

"*It runs good!*"

"*What?*" she yelled, idling back so she could hear me.

"It runs good," I repeated.

"What did you expect!" She gestured for me to climb on the seat behind her. She took a pair of goggles out of her pocket and put them on. "Hang on," she said. I put my arms around her waist and we took off fast, kicking up a thin, brisk trail of dirt.

For the next few moments I forgot about the danger Skip was in, or who had kidnapped him, or where we were

135

going. It was all I could do to hold on as we blasted by the cemetery at about thirty miles per hour.

"Going downhill is my favorite part!" Miss Eddie Mack yelled at me.

"What?" I could barely hear her.

"Never mind!" she shouted.

We started up Grand Avenue, and it was just as Miss Eddie Mack had predicted: people along the way stared at us as if we'd dropped down from the sky.

I guess we *were* an unusual sight: the great-grand-daughter of the town "Witch" roaring up Main Street on a red motor scooter with a condemned, twelve-year-old practical joker hanging on for dear life. When we went by my house I hoped my parents didn't see us. But I have to admit, even though I knew I was stretching my family's loyalty pretty thin, I was kind of proud to be where I was.

As luck would have it, Mama and Daddy came out of the house to get into the car just as we roared by. I feigned not to see them and looked straight ahead as if I went riding with Miss Eddie Mack every last day of my life.

When we passed Rivers' house she ran down from the front porch and waved in astonishment. I saw Bubba and Henjie and Billy playing marbles in Henjie's driveway. They couldn't believe their eyes. Percy was just coming out of his barn when we passed him. He scratched his head like he was having visions. All in all, we left an impenetrable trail of incredulous faces in our wake.

Now that I'd gotten a little more accustomed to riding on the motorscooter I began to wonder again where we were going. We sped a few miles out of town and Miss Eddie Mack turned off the paved state highway onto a dirt road. We must've gone several miles, because I could see the river out in the distance.

"There's somebody following us," she said ominously.

I looked back and saw a pickup truck turning onto the dirt road behind us.

136

"Can you make them out?" she said.

"There's too much dust," I shouted. All I could see were two men's silhouettes in the cab of the pursuing truck. They looked big.

Miss Eddie Mack turned down a farm road between the expansive flat cotton fields. The ghostly truck was like a specter; it remained on our trail but kept its distance. I was certain now that someone was really following us. My chest grew tight and I could hardly breathe. Until now it had all seemed an inconsequential little game. All of a sudden it was as real as the bloody feathers and chickens' heads and black candle stubs I'd found scattered in the forest.

"*Go*, Miss Eddie Mack!" I yelled.

"I'm wide open," she called, "but my top speed's only about thirty-five. *Hang on!*"

She jerkily swerved off the dirt road and cut through a cotton field between the rows. I glanced back and saw the mysterious truck circling the field on a lane made for the cultivators and tractors. They were trying to block us off before we reached the woods.

I felt the cotton plants whip against my ankles. It had to have hurt but for some reason I didn't feel anything. Over Miss Eddie Mack's shoulder I saw the looming woods ahead. We were almost there. Once in the trees, however, we'd have to stop and make a run for it. How fast could Miss Eddie Mack run?

Then I wondered where we were heading. My companion steered onto an old cow trail that ran through the trees, not wide enough for a car or truck but passable for a motorscooter. The trail was badly overgrown, but we were able to bump along over the occasional clumps of grass and sticks and dead limbs. At our clamorous approach frightened swarms of birds cried out and rose from the trees and madly flew away into the sky. I could hardly blame them. I looked back again and saw the truck skid to a halt at the

137

edge of the woods. I heard a door slam shut, but the trees were too thick to see who it was.

The path wound treacherously among the trees and gradually straightened out. We gathered speed and put distance between us and whoever was after us. I sighed in relief but kept watching over her shoulder in the event we hit a tree. The trail led now up a hill and down a gentle slope, across a shallow, rippling stream, one of the gloomy little tributary creeks that eventually emptied into the river. Miss Eddie Mack blasted over the rocky streambed, scattering a white sheet of spray on either side. The water felt good in the face.

Suddenly the trail emerged from the woods onto yet another unceremonious dirt road. She turned onto it and accumulated speed again. From the sun at our backs I could tell that we were headed west. I'd never been on this road before, but she seemed to know precisely where she was going. We were moving deeper and deeper into a low swampy terrain that bordered the river. Giant cypress trees towered overhead, and thick green vines were tangled in the shadowy underbrush.

Miss Eddie Mack slowed down and carefully surveyed the left side of the road until she found a timber trail made by the pulpwood trucks. She turned onto it. For about ten minutes we followed this trail until it became too overgrown to go any farther. She suddenly applied the brakes and turned off the motor when the trail ended in a gumtree thicket choked with big, thorny brambles. We got off and I helped her push the machine behind a bush so that it was completely hidden from sight.

"Come on," she said, pulling off her goggles.

"Where are we going?"

"You'll see when we get there."

I ducked under a long, heavy branch that Miss Eddie Mack held aside for me. "Who do you think was following us?" I asked.

138

"Whoever it was, was up to no good."

We climbed a long, shallow ridge through a formidable pine copse, our footfalls deadened by thick pinestraw so that we moved noiselessly, like animals of the forest. Miss Eddie Mack was marvelously agile for someone her age—she could've been 60 or 70; I never was any good at guessing a lady's age—but by the time we reached the crest of the ridge she was straining for breath.

She held up a warning hand, and then I saw what she was looking at. In a murky clearing some sixty or seventy yards below us was a half-deteriorated shotgun cabin and some unpainted outbuildings, a shed and a barn and a privy with a half moon carved out of its door. Two trucks and a van were parked near the cabin. Off to the side were derelict, rusted hulks of old cars and trucks and a steam-operated tractor with weeds grown up all around them as though they'd been there for many years. A man was sitting on the porch in a rocking chair, with a rifle propped against the wall. He wore soiled overalls and was oddly motionless, his head carelessly slumped forward. Then I saw a bottle in his hand and guessed he was drunk.

"That's Spit McGee's daddy!" I said. "And there's *Spit!*"

Spit himself came out the side door of the cabin carrying a pan of food. He glanced at his father as if he didn't want to be seen, then slipped soundlessly, on bare and nimble feet, inside the barn.

"He helps them run their still," Miss Eddie Mack said.

"You mean, I was right?" I said. "But *Spit?*" The awareness of it killed me.

"Shhhh, keep your voice down. When Spit showed you how to paint that witch's sign on the Clark Mansion he was creating a *diversion*. That gave the moonshiners the idea of playing on the town's fear of witches and disguising where they were setting up their stills. But, Willie, these are dangerous men. It's not just Spit's daddy. These are *killers*."

"Who are they?" I asked. Before Miss Eddie Mack could reply, another man came out of the barn rudely dragging Spit by the collar of his shirt. He was the tallest man I ever saw. He must've been seven feet tall, and cruelty rose from him like a beastly predator. He wore a slouch hat with the brim pulled over his face, so I couldn't see what he looked like, except that he had long, jet-black hair protruding from under his floppy hat. He shoved Spit in the direction of the woodpile and kicked at him. Spit grudgingly picked up an ax and started chopping wood, but when the big man turned his back Spit gave him a mean dirty look.

"That tall one's part Indian," Miss Eddie Mack whispered. "Descendant of the Yazoo Indians who were dispossessed by white settlers in the early eighteen-hundreds. Every generation of them's sought revenge in some way. Some deep instinct keeps bringing them back to Yazoo County."

"Are they the same ones that holed up in the Clark Mansion last year?" I said intuitively. "The ones we got?"

"Either them or their cousins. Some such."

Suddenly I heard a sound that struck at my deepest heart, a yelp of unfathomable love and hope. It came from the farthest recesses of the barn, a high-pitched yapping that I knew as well as my own voice.

"*That's Skip!*" I started to get up. Miss Eddie Mack pulled me down. I struggled against her. "They've got my dog. I'm going to get him!"

"All right," Miss Eddie Mack whispered again. "Then get your dog. Maybe there's a loose board at the back of the barn that your dog can crawl through. But go slow and be quiet."

We began working our way down the slope, the two of us, keeping out of sight behind the trees and cloying brush until we reached the border of the clearing. This was ugly, shrivelled terrain, parched and taut and mean. We slowly circled around behind the barn. I put my ear to the boards

140

and listened, but there was no sound. The boards were rough and weathered but nailed solidly together. There was not a single crack in them to see through.

"I'm going around to the front," I said.

"Wait!" she said. But I was already crawling away. She grabbed at my trousers leg to stop me, but I kept going. I wanted my dog.

I squirmed around the obscured side of the barn out of view of the cabin. If I turned the corner I'd be in full view of Spit's daddy, who still sprawled comatose in the rocker on the front porch. He seemed to be sound asleep, his head still slumped forward, the whiskey bottle in his hand dragging the floor. I inched along the ground on my stomach cautiously, eyeing the silent, collapsed figure.

It was an eternity to the swinging doors. They were closed, but there was a small crack between them. I tried to look inside, but it was too dark. I leapt up and unbolted the doors, then slipped inside, hoping Spit's father hadn't seen me.

My eyes slowly adjusted to the gloom. The dusty, pungent smell of hay was permeated by a sourish sweet odor I couldn't readily identify. It smelled strangely like licorice. In the musty gloom I ascertained several stalls on one side of the barn where rows of five gallon metal cans had been stacked. The licorice odor seemed to be coming from there.

Now I could see everything: an enormous loft overhead with a trap door, and diverse items of equipment piled everywhere, pipes and metal boilers and coils of copper tubing. Then I felt something cold and wet touch my hand. It was Old Skip's nose!

"Skip!" I cried, oblivious to whether anyone else was inside this barn or not. I hugged him to me and he panted joyously in my ear, swathing my nose with his tongue. I felt his happy heart beating against mine. "Oh, Skip!"

Just then a man's shout came from outside, then the relentless scuffling of running feet. I heard Miss Eddie Mack yell, "*Run, Willie!*"

I grabbed Skip up and opened the door a crack. A third man we'd not seen had discovered Miss Eddie Mack and was chasing her into the woods. Carrying Skip in my arms I slipped around the shady side of the barn and ran right into the biggest pair of hands I'd ever seen.

They belonged to the tall ugly man with the greasy black hair sticking out from under his hat. He had a smile like a buzz saw.

"Hello, dead boy," he said.

Fifteen

MISS EDDIE MACK AND I lay in the covered van of a truck. Our hands and feet were tied and we were gagged. We were spreadeagled and at the mercy of heartless men.

The men who'd caught us had brought Skip along. Now that Skip had served his purpose—which obviously had been to lure us to them—they were content to let me have him back for the moment. He sat next to me breathing deeply in the cruel stifling heat of the van. He sensed something was wrong but didn't know what to do about it. If I'd not been gagged, I would've told Skip to jump out of the truck and run for home. Run for Daddy and Percy, run for the sheriff! But I couldn't talk. Also, one of the men was riding in the back of the truck with us.

It was dark and uncomfortably stuffy. We sat on the floor, or rather bounced on it, as the truck rattled over the holes and crevices in the road. Nearby was a small chicken coop with two clucking chickens in it. There was also a burlap bag in the far corner smelling rankly of decay. I could guess what was in it: dead animals.

The gang was undoubtedly headed for another of its stills with the intent of disguising the site as a place where the "devil worshippers" had held a sacrificial ceremony. I was so scared I couldn't think clearly. What sacrifices might these moonshiners have in mind?

Finally, after what must've been many miles, the truck came to a halt. The rear doors swung open, and the tall man stood outlined against the blazing glare of the sun. We were pulled roughly outside. I glanced around to see if I recognized where we were. Behind us was another logging trail, but it wasn't the same one I'd followed with Ollie the day he showed me the second sacrificial place. All I knew was that we were deep in the woods– and deep in trouble.

The big arbitrary man dragged both of us down a path through the trees until we came to a narrow red ravine. They pulled us behind them like animals. I could feel the skin scraping off my back. The path led down into the gulley, which we followed until it widened out in a flat, partly open space where the still had been set up. Tall pines formed a canopy of verdant camouflage overhead. I heard the lazy drone of an airplane and looked up expectantly but couldn't spot the aircraft.

Two other strange men were busy disassembling the still, taking apart the copper tubing, disconnecting tubes from the enormous boilers on an iron frame above the burnt remnants of logs. They'd left Spit and his daddy behind. Spit's father probably had been too drunk to come along.

A mental image flashed in my mind of the other Satanic spots I'd seen. This one was uncannily identical, right down to the placement of the fire pit and the firewood stacked nearby.

The big man pushed Miss Eddie Mack and me to the

ground and bound our feet together more tightly. Skip lay down beside me, whining sympathetically. The tall man and the silent one who'd guarded us in the back of the truck went to fetch the chicken coop and the burlap bag. At the slightest move my bonds cut my wrists. I felt blood flowing onto my palms. Miss Eddie Mack's wrists were bleeding, too. My tongue was dry and the gag hurt the corners of my mouth. I was so tense I throbbed all over. I could barely move. I glanced frantically at Miss Eddie Mack, and she *winked* at me.

That wink spoke to me, saying loud and clear across the desperation: Don't lose hope.

I relaxed a little, enough to take stock of what our torturers looked like. They would've made good Nazis. They were the meanest-looking people I ever saw, with grim vacuous faces and dark stolid eyes. They wore dirty blue jeans or khaki work clothes; they went about their work without saying much to each other. All three of them looked strong and powerful. They ignored Miss Eddie Mack and me. We could just as well have been a couple of logs tossed thoughtlessly to the ground. In fact, our captors seemed to have forgotten we existed, which could be either a good or bad sign, depending on how you looked at it.

One of the men, the one taking apart the still, was obese and redfaced, with sandy hair and freckles, and pendulous ears like rusty doorknobs. If he was a descendant of the Yazoo Indians, it had to have been a flawed geneology—from a Scottish or Irish branch of that embittered tribe. His partner, who helped him carry the heavy boiler to the truck, had light brown hair balding at the back and a sallow, pallid complexion. He was no Indian either. The only one of them who looked like he could've been descended from the legendary giants was the tall cruel man with jet-black hair. He exuded hate.

He was certainly big enough. He carried the wooden chicken coop in *one* hand. He took the chickens from the

145

coop, held them up, and wrung their necks with a casual flip of his wrist, carelessly tossing them flapping to the tawdry, ambiguous ground one upon the other. The whole business only took a few seconds, the poor creatures scarcely squawking as they departed this life. Their wings continued to beat after they were dead. The other man dumped out the contents of the burlap bag. Two dead animals thumped to the ground. They were possums, eyes wide and glassy.

I watched in disbelief as the two men efficiently dismembered the chickens and dropped the fresh blood all around, then scattered the parts and feathers across the immediate area. They withdrew several black candle stubs from their pockets and placed them in a circle.

Here, then, were Yazoo's "devil worshippers." There were no sacrificial virgins, no flickering fires, no masks nor chants nor dancing, no flutes nor drums nor screams in the night: only the quick, proficient dismantling of a portable distillery and the equally meticulous, emotionless dismembering of helpless animals. The tall man and his partner chatted lightly with each other. They could've been assembly line workers. I hated them one and all.

"How did they find us?" the big man said. He was shoveling dirt into the firepit. I'd heard the other men call him "Tiny." His voice was hoarse and gutteral, like a rumble of thunder.

"I reckon they walked up to the cabin," the second man, whom the others called Elroy, replied nonchalantly. "They must've come on foot or we would've heard their motor. It don't matter how they got there anyhow, not now."

I realized they were talking about Miss Eddie Mack and me. This was unsettling to say the least.

"You damn fool, it does too matter!" Tiny muttered. "We got to git rid of their vehicle, don't we? They didn't *walk* fifteen miles from town."

Elroy said nothing. If he minded being called a damn

146

fool, he wasn't about to make much of anything out of it with somebody that was seven feet tall.

"I reckon we can get 'em to tell us how they come," he said, his tone so acrid and menacing it set my teeth on edge.

"That reminds me," Tiny said, angrily kicking ashes and burnt ends of logs over the mound of dirt to disguise the firepit. "Did we ever decide how devil worshippers kill their victims?"

"Slit their throat, I guess," Elroy replied.

I glanced at Miss Eddie Mack in horror, and she calmly shook her head. I wished I knew where her dauntlessness came from.

"No, no," Tiny argued, "they always hold a knife over-head with both hands–like this–and plunge it downward through *here*." He pointed to the base of his neck, just above the collarbone. "And don't do it quick. Just make 'em *suffer*."

"I don't think it matters," the other said. "I mean, what if one of the sacrifices tried to *run,* and you had to do the job everwhich way you could? I bet that happens all the time. Probably happens that way a lot in Arkansas."

"They don't sacrifice humans all the time, you clod!" Tiny grumbled. "We got to do it just right if the fools around here are gonna accept this as a devil worshippers' killin', 'specially after that Belzoni man got up and told his story to the whole town. We got a lot of money ridin' on this. How much money we got in that Memphis bank? Didn't I get that Latin from that rich man in Memphis? Maybe we ought to rethink the situation."

"Hey, Buster!" Elroy called ironically to the redfaced blond man. "Tiny is rethinkin' the situation!"

Buster came over and began to argue with Tiny about our fate while Miss Eddie Mack and I listened, bound and gagged and at their terrible mercy.

"We can't be changin' horses in the middle of the stream,"

147

Buster said. He apparently wasn't too afraid of Tiny. "We decided on a plan. Now let's do it."

"It won't work," Tiny said.

"See what I mean?" Elroy said to Buster.

"Whatta you mean, it won't work?" Buster was enraged, but he shoved his hands into his pockets to show Tiny he was not *that* enraged.

"The law won't buy it," Tiny said. His voice seemed to vibrate up from the bowels of the earth. His eyes were like ashen coals. "That sheriff won't buy the sacrifice idea."

"How do you know?" Buster said.

"I said, it won't work. I ain't gonna say it again."

"Okay," Buster said, suddenly humble. He'd seen the mean cast of Tiny's features.

"Whatever you say, Tiny!" Elroy added.

"I been thinkin'," Tiny went on. "We can take them to that old plantation house, the one that McGee used to live in. If we put some devil signs around–candles and feathers and bones and stuff–we can make it look like the cult was out there havin' a ceremony until they had a accident..."

"What kind of accident?" Buster asked.

"They burned the house down, and two of 'em got crisped." Tiny turned and looked down at us, and at Old Skip lying frightened by my side. His gaunt cheekbones and deepset eyes resembled a living skull, a death's head on a seven-foot chassis.

"Yeah," Buster said.

"Yeah!" Elroy said.

Having decided our fate in such plebescite fashion, they resumed clearing the area and packing their equipment. There was something terrible about the way they walked complacently back and forth in an unwavering straight line, like worker ants. I glanced again at Miss Eddie Mack and saw fear in her eyes for the first time. I felt sorry for her, almost as sorry as I did for myself.

All my nightmares crushed in on me. The clicking sound

148

I heard was my own teeth chattering. I'd never get to see the Cardinals play. I'd never go to New York. I'd never kiss Rivers. Bound and spreadeagled like valueless beasts, Miss Eddie Mack and I awaited our fate. Skip curled up against me and put his head in my lap. Tears welled in my eyes, and I turned my head away so Miss Eddie Mack wouldn't notice.

Ten feet from where I lay a vision swam into view. I blinked my eyes rapidly. I thought I'd seen Spit McGee behind a pine tree! In my anguished fever was I dreaming?

The men came to get us then, and as Buster grabbed me savagely and threw me over his shoulder, I twisted my head and looked at the spot where I thought I'd seen Spit. His face appeared again, just for an instant.

It *was* Spit! Even upside down I knew that narrow face with the wide grin and straw-colored hair and close-set eyes anywhere.

Good old Spit, I thought as I bounced on Buster's hard angular shoulder: my dear friend, my valued associate and fishing partner. What a good old boy.

Spit, Spit, he's my man. If he can't do it, nobody can.

But do what? Tiny was carrying Miss Eddie Mack right behind me. She looked like a trussed doll in his hands. How I hated these strong, heartless creatures! They dumped us into the back of the truck as before and pushed us farther inside with the heels of their boots. That gives you an idea of how much they regarded us. Then in afterthought they tossed Skip inside like a rag.

How had Spit gotten there? Had he found our motor-scooter? Would he go to the nearest telephone and call the sheriff? I relayed psychic messages to Spit as hard as I could. I tensed my whole agonized body and *pushed* extra-sensory perceptions out to Spit. As Tiny started the engine and turned the truck around I listened in vain for the sound of a motorscooter down in the woods, but we were too far away to hear.

149

The truck bounced along the rutted logging trail until it reached the dirt road, then picked up speed. We seemed to be going much faster than before. Maybe I was imagining it. Our sallow-faced guard, Elroy, grinned at me brutally. I leaned back against the side of the van and tried to breathe normally, to slow the thumping of my all-suffering heart. Miss Eddie Mack's face was starkly pale, her grey hair stuck out crazily in all directions, like some cartoon character with her finger in an electrical socket. Yet even then her proud face remained stubbornly determined. To my dying day I'd never forget the look of her in that moment, although my dying day was now.

She too seemed to be concentrating with all her might. She was staring straight ahead but not looking at anything in particular. She appeared instead to be withdrawing inside herself.

The truck stopped with a sudden jolt. Tiny threw open the metal doors and lifted me out with one hand. Buster was there to hoist me over his shoulder again, while Tiny carried Miss Eddie Mack. Just before my view was obstructed by Buster's broad back, I caught a glimpse of the Clark Mansion.

The ruined old house stood in the late afternoon's sun looking placid and ordinary, familiar and funny and strange all at once. The witch's star had faded so that it was almost invisible. But it had done its job, starting the insane wheels of destiny into motion. I wished with all my being I could go back in time and erase the sign, but now it was too late. Would it hurt to die? I missed my Mama. I missed Rivers. Dying would hurt!

When Buster carried me through the open door I caught a sidelong glimpse of a solitary bluejay flying out a broken window. In an inflamed, crazy way it was like coming home.

Inside, Buster and Tiny dumped us on the rotten floorboards as though we were sacks of feed. My shoulder ached from where I hit the floor. Miss Eddie Mack cried out beneath her gag and then was silent. I hoped she hadn't broken any bones.

I raised my head and looked around me. From my low perspective the room looked huge. Overhead the rafters were exposed where the scavengers had torn away the ceiling boards. There was a hole in the rotten floor that Bubba had fallen through that night a year ago, and discarded old mattresses where Spit and his father had slept, and pyramids of dust the termites had contrived, and cobwebs stretching in spectral shimmers across the corners. My mind took in all these details with a horrid clarity, while at the same time fear kept swooshing around me like a meteor.

Let's see, I thought, the Cushman Flyer has a top speed of 35 mph. How long would it take Spit to find a country store somewhere? Would the store have a telephone? *Swoosh.* Had Spit returned to the gang's cabin instead, to warn his father to get out? *Swoosh.* Before the gang committed murder? Whose murder? *Swoosh* went the meteor. *Swoosh, swoosh, swoosh.*

Then I heard a splashing sound. The unmistakable smell of gasoline permeated the deteriorated room. All my life I'd smelled gas at my daddy's service station. Sometimes he'd let me work the pumps and wash the windshields. He paid me a nickel a car. Gasoline had always been a friendly smell, an odor of commerce and benevolence, of helping folks get where they were going to. Now it was the smell of death. The giant sadist Tiny was sprinkling the gasoline along the splintery baseboards. He pointedly sloshed some on my tennis shoes. I jerked my bound feet away, but it was too late for that. Old Skip squirmed closer to me. I prayed that he'd get up and leave. They were through with him. At least *he* could survive. But he stayed with me. One match would set everything

151

blazing—walls, floor and me, and Miss Eddie Mack and Old Skip.

Tiny went to the door and yelled to Buster and Elroy: "Stay clear!"

Then he dug in his pockets for matches. His glance swept the room, passing coldly over Miss Eddie Mack and Skip and me as if we were part of the obsolete furniture. I made a muffled sound, trying to signal to Miss Eddie Mack. When the inferno started, if we rolled over we might somehow manage to reach a window. She didn't seem to hear me. She was staring straight ahead with that fierce, unbroken, riveting concentration. What was she thinking at a time like this?

The loathesome Tiny reached in his hip pockets, then patted his shirt pockets.

"Anybody got a match?" he called out the door with a crazy caveman's leer. The grin froze on his face, and hope welled up in me like an atomic cloud.

"Come out of the house with your hands in the air!"

The words came from outside. It had a metallic echo that made it super-human. Then I recognized Lieutenant McDowell's voice, amplified mightily through a bullhorn.

Tiny ducked away from the open door. His hand dipped into his hip pocket and a switchblade knife appeared as by magic. I heard scuffling noises outside, then the sharp reports of gunfire. Tiny ran bent over to where I was lying and dragged me back to the door with him. He pushed me into view, into the line of fire. I tried to yell through my gag, "Don't shoot!" But all that came out was "Oh-ooh!"

"Hold your fire!" the lieutenant said over his bullhorn.

I saw Buster lying face down in the weeds. Elroy was pinned against the side of their truck by the sheriff's deputy, who was handcuffing his hands behind his scruffy back. Then I saw the lieutenant standing behind another pickup truck. Was it the same one that had followed Miss

Eddie Mack and me? He had his bullhorn in one hand and a .38 pistol in the other.

In that instant I saw Spit McGee again. He was standing at the other end of the truck, and when he saw me he waved. I couldn't believe it. What did he expect me to do—wave back?

Tiny snatched me up and held me against him. He didn't smell very good. I felt the blade of his knife against my throat.

"Back off or I'll kill the boy and the woman!" he shouted.

The lieutenant hesitated, then holstered his pistol, raised his hand to show Tiny that he'd done so and signaled his men to move back. The sheriff and his deputy took Elroy with them, however. Buster hadn't moved. I glanced around and saw Miss Eddie Mack staring straight ahead in her intractible trance. I wondered if maybe she'd had a stroke and couldn't walk or speak. If so, I could scarcely blame her.

Tiny shoved me back inside. His insane gaze swept the room. What was he looking for? Then his eyes fixed on something. I followed his glance. Spit McGee's daddy had left a box of matches on the table next to a burned out candle stuck in a whiskey bottle. Tiny moved with me toward the table.

Miss Eddie Mack's head jerked up and she looked at him with her slicing intensity. Her eyes were like tiny pinpoints of flame. Tiny picked up the box of matches, turned around, took one step toward us—and the floor caved in beneath him!

He was trapped in the rotten floorboards up to his waist. The matchbox had fallen just outside his reach. He struggled to pull himself loose and bellowed in pain as the jagged boards cut into his sorry stomach.

There was no time to lose. I nudged Miss Eddie Mack into desperate motion and together we crawled on our sides toward the door, using our bound elbows and knees

153

to propel us along. Old Skip caught my shirt in his mouth and was trying to pull me out. A board hit the doorframe just above my head and glanced off at an angle. Tiny was throwing lumber at us, boards, the Coca-Cola box Spit's daddy had used for a stool, the remnants of a sewing machine, anything he could reach.

Then he remembered the matches. He managed to stretch forward just far enough to grab the box. I pushed Miss Eddie Mack through the door with my body. Her trousers caught on a nail. I heard matches rattle in the box, then the scratch of one of them being struck. I gathered all the strength left in me and used my head to butt Miss Eddie Mack through the door. Then I reeled into a helpless somersault just as a great fiery explosion of hot wicked air blasted me outside.

I rolled after Miss Eddie Mack onto the porch. Nothing would make me leave her. I felt something holding me by the foot, as if a jagged-toothed animal was biting deeply into me. Then I realized my shoe was on fire. I'd never felt such pain. From far away I heard my own cry. I was kicking both feet together, screaming through my gag, vaguely aware of figures running toward us. Then someone wrapped a coat around my foot and extinguished the flames. A huge fireball was rolling pell mell inside the house, bouncing from wall to wall as the Clark Mansion blazed upward like a fragile piece of tinder. Miss Eddie Mack and Skip and I lay together on the porch, helpless and smoking. We could've been dead.

The lieutenant and a deputy carried us to safety. They untied us and pulled off our gags. I started babbling to them about stills and chicken feathers and bones and motorscooters. To this day I don't really know *what* I said. I was laughing and crying at the same time. Old Skip stood at my side. He seemed to be laughing and crying too. And the other deputies were tending to Miss Eddie Mack. In my awful pain I vaguely remember bending down and hugging her, putting her face to mine.

The Clark Mansion by now had become completely engulfed in the licking, exploding flames. Tongues of fire burst up through the hole in the roof that the big oak tree had made, where the outsized limb had grown into the house and lifted the roof up. As the flames shot out through the hole, the oak swayed as if it was trying to lean away from the blaze and save itself.

I heard an engine revving and glanced around in time to see my parents' green Desoto screeching frenziedly to a halt. My Daddy jumped out and sprinted across the field toward us.

He was running like I'd always imagined him when he was young and played semi-pro ball in Tennessee—head up, legs pumping, stretching out in full stride to catch a deep fly to centerfield, determined to deny a home run. And Percy was right behind him.

Sixteen

"AND SO WE HAVE gathered here today," the mayor said, "to honor two persons, two *citizens* of Yazoo, for displaying courage and heroism beyond the call of duty which led to the capture of the criminal and murderous gang which terrorized this town and county."

I glanced self-consciously at Miss Eddie Mack, who sat next to me on the stage of the Yazoo High auditorium. She seemed unaffected by this extravagant praise, although she did hold her bouquet of roses rather stiffly. This could've been because the flowers were store-bought and not raised naturally like the kind she was used to, but I doubt it. She hadn't especially dressed up for the occasion, however, but wore her favorite short-sleeved khaki army shirt, leather vest, dark blue skirt, and brogans. Her principal concession to fashion was that she'd taken off her straw hat.

Everybody in town seemed to be there. My parents were sitting on the front row, and Percy too. Bubba and Billy and

Henjie were there. Rivers was smiling a smile just for me. Ollie was there with his little brothers and sisters sitting on the far back row. On the stage behind us was the band ensemble, which had just finished playing some Sousa marches.

I'd hoped Spit might show up, seeing as how he'd gone for help that day. The judge had sentenced Spit's daddy to nine months at Parchman, the state penitentiary, but Spit got off on good behavior because of coming forward to give evidence. He probably was out in the swampy bottoms right now, setting trotlines or curing rabbit tobacco. And I wondered if we'd ever really see him again. A juncture had been passed, I guess.

Miss Abbott didn't come to see us get our medals either, but I didn't miss her. Not one bit.

Newspaper reporters and the famous columnist Mr. Orley Hood had come from the capital city and had taken our pictures for the *Clarion-Ledger*—mine and Miss Eddie Mack's—with the mayor, the sheriff, and the lieutenant from the Mississippi Bureau of Investigation.

"Some perspective is needed for us to put these unusual events behind us," the mayor was saying. "And I'll call on Lieutenant McDowell to explain the facts of the case."

The lieutenant grinned at us as he went to the podium.

"It seems I do more public speaking than police work here in Yazoo. I don't know why that is. At any rate, what was going on was basically that a massive distillery operation was being moved around the county just a step ahead of us. And they were supplying a twelve-county radius with their foul brew. And accumulating a fortune for themselves too. The sites had been disguised to look like a ceremony of some kind was taking place there. The fact is, there was never any witches' coven or cult of any kind operating in this area. And as you all know, the case was broken with the help of Willie, here, and Mrs. Edwina

McBride. Even if their help was–" He glanced at us with amusement. "–rather unorthodox."

The lieutenant returned to his seat, and the mayor rose dramatically to make the awards. I dreaded this part, since we were supposed to make acceptance speeches. Also, I had a big bandage on my scorched foot, where I'd had a brief operation and still had a pair of crutches, and it was itching badly, but I couldn't bend down and scratch it in front of everybody.

"We have these little medallions with a Y embossed on them," the mayor said, holding up the medals as though people could see them at that distance, "and certificates of outstanding achievement for these distinguished citizens. Mrs. McBride, would you please come forward?"

Miss Eddie Mack put her roses in her chair and sauntered up to the mayor. He presented her with the medallion and certificate and stepped back so she could say what she wanted.

It was singularly quiet now, for the moment was a historic one. The town had ostracized Miss Eddie Mack for so long, people naturally expected her to use this opportunity to seek a little retribution. Her family had gotten pretty short shrift starting back in 1904, and she'd never have a better chance than this.

She just stood there looking at the printed certificate in its special folder and weighing the medallion in her hand. Then she looked at the audience. The people of Yazoo waited with solemn, wide-eyed expressions.

"I didn't do anything to deserve an award like this," she said, speaking in her droll and laconic way. "I just went to help Willie get his dog back."

A short burst of relieved laughter came from the crowd.

"If the mayor sees fit to honor me for that," she continued, "then I thank him and whoever else was behind this. But I would a durn sight rather have had some help the night those so-and-so's burned a cross in my front yard."

158

Now the audience braced themselves. So did I, a little, even though I was enjoying it.

"A lot of people," she said, "may have thought I had something to do with the so-called devil worshippers. There may have been some who thought that when a cross was burned on my property I deserved it. Well, that's all right. It doesn't matter what people say. It's the truth that matters. I don't ask much of my fellow man because I like to be independent, but out of all this I found something a lot more important than medals and awards and getting my picture in the paper." She turned and gave me that brief, elfin grin of hers, half-smile, half-grimace. "I found a friend."

She sat down before anybody had time to applaud. Then Mama started clapping, and Daddy, and Percy, and then everybody joined in, including me. Miss Eddie Mack held her roses and gave me a wink that made me feel mighty special.

Now it was my turn. The mayor called me over to receive my awards. I accepted them as slowly as possible, having completely forgotten anything to say. I was so nervous my ears felt like they were twitching. Then I looked out at the rows of faces and saw an old man dozing on the back row. What's the point of stage fright if part of your audience is already asleep?

"I'm sorry if I caused any trouble," I said, "but I guess it turned out all right." Everybody laughed and I felt better. People sure are fickle, I thought. They're with you one second, and against you the next. Maybe people just can't help it, but they sure are funny. "Oh, my mother told me to thank the mayor for saying anything nice about me." The audience interrupted with another boisterous laugh. "I'd also like to thank the sheriff and Lieutenant McDowell and somebody else." I looked out over the audience until I found him. "If Ollie Caruthers hadn't shown me the deserted places where the moonshiners had been running a

159

still, I wouldn't have known about them. Ollie, I appreciate it. And you sure can hit my curve ball."

I started clapping and everybody joined in. Ollie stood up quickly and then sat right back down, but his parents were beaming and his brothers and sisters cheered for him. Rivers was clapping for all she was worth.

"And I'd like to thank Miss Eddie Mack," I went on. "She's got a great motorscooter and...and she makes the best herb tea in Yazoo! She did a lot more than just help me get my dog Skip back, I guarantee you that. Oh, and the sheriff said he hoped I learned my lesson about playing jokes and stuff, and I guess I have. Well, that's about it."

I started to return to my seat and the audience gave a few tentative claps of applause, and then I remembered something and stepped back to the podium.

"And I'm real glad Bubba and Henjie and Billy and me don't have to go to summer school!" I said, and darted for my seat.

Seventeen

ALL OF A SUDDEN it was over.

One day I was receiving my outstanding citizen's award and the next I was putting my medallion and certificate in my bureau drawer and petting Skip on the head and asking him what we were going to do that afternoon.

Was this what being a hero was all about? I felt like a kitten in a tree. It was great going up but how did you get down? I guess I was finally growing up.

I got on my bike and went for a ride. I wound up going to Miss Eddie Mack's house accidentally on purpose. She was working in her yard transplanting flowers with a spade. I parked my bike next to the privet hedge and went to talk to her.

"Hey, Willie," she said. "You want a cup of my world-famous herbal tea?"

"No, ma'am, not right now," I said, "but there *is* something I'd like to know."

"Shoot," she said, brushing her hair back with one hand and leaving a smidgen of dirt on her forehead.

"You *winked* at me that time they had us all tied up. I was scared to death, myself," I said, but what I really meant was, What's a little old lady got that I don't?

Her leprechaun's grin came and went, quick as a summer sparrow.

"That's easy," she said. "I remembered what one of the bootleggers asked the other, about how we got there. I realized the truck that was following us was not driven by one of them. It had to be that lieutenant from Jackson. Don't be giving me more credit than I deserve. I was scared, too. Oh, boy, was I! Let's don't do it again anytime soon."

"Well, what about when that man Tiny was about to light the gasoline and burn us all up? What were you thinking about? Did you *make* him fall through the floor? Can you *do* that?"

She poked at the ground with her spade, then leaned on it and glanced at me mysteriously. I remembered how her eyes had looked at the Clark Mansion that day–pinpoints of fire–and I shivered a little with the memory. It was amazing how clear and intelligent her eyes were, now, like no eyes I'd ever seen.

"I don't know whether I can do something like that or not," she said at last, "whether it runs in the family. But I'll tell you one thing, Willie. I tried my darnedest."

We smiled at each other, then she started digging again.

"Miss Eddie Mack," I said, "I sure am glad you're on my side."

I got on my bike and pedaled back down the hill past the cemetery. Skip loped along beside me. A warm breeze came blowing out of the Delta and swept across old Yazoo.

Something about the town had changed. The streets led off at familiar angles that I knew so well; the houses and trees sat in their usual places looking back at me like old comrades; I recognized nearly every person I saw. And yet

162

everything seemed different. It would be a long time before I realized that Yazoo hadn't changed. It was I who was changing. I was beginning to look beyond the hills and the Delta toward something else, but I was in no hurry to find it.

I heard a car horn honking. Bubba turned the corner in his Model-A. Rivers and Billy and Henjie were with him. I stopped on the sidewalk and waited for them to catch up with me. Since that day at the sheriff's office we'd sort of started over again with each other. It wasn't easy, but we'd been friends too long not to try. I guess we'd shared too much, and remembered. And maybe that's what really matters. Bubba braked the roadster sharply, and Rivers laughed.

"Hey, Willie," he called, "want to get a moonpie and an R.C. and ride around?"

"Don't mind if I do," I said.

I left my bike in somebody's yard. Skip and I piled in the car and we went driving off, keeping mostly to the alleys in case we ran into the police. Rivers smiled at me and secretly squeezed my hand. Now that we were going into the eighth grade she'd started acting different toward me, in a strangely tender and determined way that gave me goosebumps. I could see that life was about to get complicated.

In the meantime, the marshmellow filling of a moonpie tasted as good as it always had; an R.C. was as deeply satisfying as ever; and Old Skip was still the only dog in the world that could drive a car.

Bubba turned up Main Street and when we got close to Jones Feed and Seed he hunched down in the seat with Skip standing in his lap, forepaws propped on the steering wheel. There wasn't much traffic, and the old men sitting on the benches in front of the feed store couldn't miss us. But just to make sure, Bubba tooted the horn. One of the

163

senior citizens pointed at us and the others looked up, shook their heads, and went back to their whittling.

"Shoot, Willie, nobody's lookin'!" Bubba said.

"There was a time," Henjie said philosophically, "when they'd have thrown down their walkin' sticks and run after the car."

"They're spoiled by too much excitement," Rivers said.

"You know, things are startin' to get borin' again," Billy said.

"That's okay with me," I said.

The End